BED & BREAKFAST BEDLAM

BED & BREAKFAST BEDLAM

Book I

Abby Vandiver

Bed & Breakfast Bedlam is a work of fiction. Any
references or similarities to actual events,
organizations, real people - living, or dead, or to real
locales are intended to give the novel a sense of
reality. All other events and characters portrayed are
a product of the author's imagination or are used
fictitiously.

For more, visit my website: www.abbyvandiver.com
Follow me on Twitter: @AbbyVandiver
Facebook: www.facebook.com/authorabbyl.vandiver

ISBN-13: 978-1521726-1-8-1
Cover Design by Shondra C. Longino

First Printing June 2015
Printed in the United States

To m

Prologue

Every day is the first day of the rest of your life.

Or so the saying goes. But most times, I'd say ninety-nine percent of the time, your life goes pretty much as you plan it – or don't plan it. Mundane everyday sort of stuff. You go to college, get married, have kids – or not. On a small scale the daily happenings in a person's life are pretty much inconsequential and certainly not leading to anything monumental. But when viewed through the backdrop of history, sometimes, some of those insignificant, trivial day-to-day kinds of things have colossal after-effects.

For instance, the Archduke Ferdinand deciding to visit injured patients at a local hospital, and Gravilo Princip just happening to visit a certain café at the same time. Those innocuous decisions ultimately led

BED & BREAKFAST BEDLAM

Book I

Abby Vandiver

For more, visit my website: www.abbyvandiver.com
Follow me on Twitter: @AbbyVandiver
Facebook: www.facebook.com/authorabbyl.vandiver

ISBN-13: 978-1521726-1-8-1
Cover Design by Shondra C. Longino

First Printing June 2015
Printed in the United States

10 9 8 7 6 5 4 3 2 1

Dedication

To my granddaughter, Sydne, my redheaded road dog.

to Princip assassinating Ferdinand and the start of World War I.

Or, the small chunk of debris innocently traveling through space that found Planet Earth in its path a few million years ago. It, in a one-in-four-hundred-billion chance, struck in the exact spot where its impact could cause the extinction of all the dinosaurs (although my mother has a different theory about that), making us have to spend tens of years and tens of thousands of dollars to dig them up just to find out what they looked like.

Archaeologists, like me, mark time around such events. Like BCE or AD (before the Common Era, although I prefer Before Christ denoted as BC, and *Anno Domini*). Or like denoting an age, or period (like Victorian and Jurassic). Usually though, such history marking events happen over long periods, and are not classified as distinct times in our history until long after they occur.

But for me, the mammoth event that completely changed the course of my history, happened over the period of just one week. And it only took me one day to realize it.

What marked the complete and utter change in the course of my ordinary life? It was the death of a total stranger.

Chapter One
Track Rock Gap
Gainesville, Georgia

Wednesday Night, BGD (Before Gemma Died)

My heart was beating out of my chest.

I stood with my back against the outside wall of a small wooden shed, sweat dripping down my face, and tried to slow down my racing heart. I knew if I didn't, the sound of it thumping would give away my position.

"How am I going to get out of this?" I muttered

I felt my legs trembling, my palms were clammy, and my whole body was reeling in a flood of fear. I bent over, resting my hands on my knees, while trying to catch my breath, and prayed. It seemed as if I could almost hear God saying in response, "That's what you get, Logan."

I should have listened to my mother.

My mother had told me not to go poking my nose (or the rest of me for that matter) into federally protected lands. But still, at nearly thirty, I had to rail against her advice just to prove I was capable of managing my life without her interference.

Look where that got me.

I peeked my head around the shed and tried to focus my eyes through the darkness.

Two U.S. Forest Service officers were shining their flashlights on the metal heap I had upended. It seemed I didn't have the criminal savvy or cat-like moves that I thought I had. Clumsy didn't even start to describe the maze of mishaps that led me to my current predicament.

I slid down the wall, crouching, I swiped the back of my hand across my forehead, and narrowed my eyes, searching for a way out.

Hopefully, there was one.

I was at the Track Rock Gap ruins in Gainesville, Georgia. I had been here before – on the other side of the locked gate – as an archaeologist looking for ancient Maya ruins with my mother.

At some point, thousands of years ago, the Maya population disappeared from Central America. Many archaeologists believed that they died *en masse*. But being more like my mother than I ever cared to admit, I had a different theory. While excavating in Belize, my mother and I discovered clues that lead us to believe that the Maya may have migrated to, and lived in, Georgia. At Track Rock Gap to be exact.

When we checked it out, word had gotten around the area that Maya ruins laid up the side of a steep mountainside inside Track Rock Gap that was comprised of more than a 150 stone masonry walls with Mayan-like inscriptions, evidence of agricultural terraces, and remains of what could have been a sophisticated irrigation system. Just like what was found in the jungles of Mesoamerica at every Maya site excavated.

But if the Maya had settled in America, the U.S. government didn't want anyone to know about it.

When my mother and I first arrived we found Track Rock Gap locked tight with big "KEEP OUT" signs plastered everywhere. So we left. My mother's scientific need to know not even stirred. Mine, however, was screaming for answers. I just had to know why anyone would keep possible proof of a Maya civilization in Georgia secret, so I decided to come and check it out – trespassing laws be damned.

Now I was being chased by two federal officers for my callous disregard of my government's edicts. And to top it off I still didn't have any more information about the Maya-American occupation I came to out.

Prologue

Every day is the first day of the rest of your life.

Or so the saying goes. But most times, I'd say ninety-nine percent of the time, your life goes pretty much as you plan it – or don't plan it. Mundane everyday sort of stuff. You go to college, get married, have kids – or not. On a small scale the daily happenings in a person's life are pretty much inconsequential and certainly not leading to anything monumental. But when viewed through the backdrop of history, sometimes, some of those insignificant, trivial day-to-day kinds of things have colossal after-effects.

For instance, the Archduke Ferdinand deciding to visit injured patients at a local hospital, and Gravilo Princip just happening to visit a certain café at the same time. Those innocuous decisions ultimately led

But, at this moment, I realized that I no longer had any interest in where they lived, whatsoever.

I'm sure that had to do with the fact that now my curiosity was going to get me thrown in jail. Or worse, a federal prison.

My recon skills were nowhere as good as my excavation ones. I hadn't been able to get a map of the area, and I came armed only with a flashlight and my iPhone 6. Neither one turned out to be any help. Before I was more than a hundred yards into the site, I had knocked over the shed. A metal one that creaked and clanked as it fell with a loud thud spitting dirt everywhere. It scared me and I took off running. As it turned out, I ran in the same direction the guards were emerging from. I did a one eighty and slid the last few feet behind the shed where I now stooped. Thank God they hadn't seen me.

I peered around the shed. The two guards were still examining the metal pile of heap. They were kicking it with the toe of their shoes.

Maybe they'd think some vermin knocked it over. Or, maybe they'd think it fell by itself. It hadn't been very sturdy. I barely touched it.

"Is anyone there? Show yourself," one of the guards yelled.

Crap.

I turned back around and closed my eyes. I knew I couldn't just stand still and let them catch me, I had to make a run for it.

Plus, I had to pee.

That was going to make running anywhere pretty difficult.

I opened my eyes to survey what was close and spotted a trailer about thirty yards out. With the light that emanated from the trailer, I could see that just beyond it was a tangle of bushes and trees. A place I could escape in darkness and the noises of the night, and through them, I hoped, was the road out.

But I needed to distract Uncle Sam's watchmen.

I closed my eyes and asked for strength. Even though my mother was a lot closer to God than I was, and I typically went against her, I was hoping He'd give me some slack.

Pulling in a quick breath and holding it, I threw a rock as hard as I could in the opposite direction of where I needed to go.

"Did you hear that?" one guard said to the other.

"What?"

"Thought I heard something over there." He pointed in the direction I threw the rock. "We'd better check it out." They took off one way and I took off running in the other.

I landed behind the small camper-like building. There was a dim light on inside. I peeped through a window and discovered that the place must be the guard station. There were two desks, some chairs, a microwave and a coffeemaker. The light I'd seen was from a computer screen.

Yep. This was where they hung out when vandals, like me, weren't on the prowl in their protected lands.

I wonder what kind of jail time federal trespassing carries? I let out a sigh.

Looked like my recognition wasn't going to come from brilliant work in the field of Maya archaeology but from my stupid mistakes off the grid. This was going to ruin my reputation as an archaeologist. The small one that I had.

I looked up at the darkened sky and thanked God there was little moonlight. Darkness was a good cover. I spied the start of the dense bushes that lined the perimeter only a few yards away, then took one more look in the direction the guards had gone. After I felt I was clear, I fell flat on my belly and slithered across the dirt and patches of grass to the trees. I rolled over on my back once I reached them, I raised up my hand at the pale moon and said softly, "I will, in no way, shape, or form, ever break the law again. I absolutely and solemnly swear."

Now to get out of Track Rock Gap and walk – *nay* – run the mile and a half down the road to where I had parked my car.

Chapter Two

Itza, Georgia

Early Thursday Morning, BGD

I settled my bill at the small motel I had stayed at first thing. After nearly getting caught trespassing the night before, I didn't want to waste any time beating it out of town. Not that I thought they knew who I was or that they could find me. Still it made me a little nervous being so close to the memory of my illegal activities.

I headed out to the parking lot, knapsack over my shoulder, pulling my luggage behind me, I walked at a brisk pace. I slowed down as I passed the glass-encased office. The door to the small room was open. Eyes straightforward, I wanted to appear calm – normal. I'd smile and wave if the clerk looked up at me. That was when I heard "him."

"Logan Dickerson," he said. "You said her name is Logan Dickerson?"

I stopped dead in my tracks.

What the hey?

"That's right. She came in last night. Covered in dirt," the woman at the counter was saying. "She looked real suspicious like."

My heart stopped. How did that woman see me come in? That little . . . toothless . . . old snoop. She had a big mouth. Telling some unknown man stuff about me. He could be a stalker. Someone out to kill me. I tried to peek through the door and get a better look at him.

Who was he anyway?

My heart started beating again – pounding actually – in my ears. It was so loud that I couldn't hear a word they were saying. So I moved in closer, stilled myself, and tilting my head I listened.

"Last night you say?" he asked.

I couldn't hear her answer, but she must have said, yes.

"What does she look like?" he asked.

Don't tell him, big mouth. Don't. Tell. Him.

"She's black, like you. Shoulder length hair. Light skinned. Not skinny. Not fat."

Crap.

"And how long has she been here?"

Was there no end to his questions?

"Two nights," the woman blabbed.

Oh my goodness, I thought. *She's gotta be breaking some kind of privacy law telling that man all my business.*

"Did she kill somebody?" Blabbermouth asked.

"No," he said and chuckled.

"Then how come the FBI is looking for her?"

FBI? Oh my God! I am going to jail.

"Where is she now?" he asked, seemingly ignoring her question.

"Don't know. Still in her room I'm guessing 'cause that's her jeep over there. The white one."

I looked over at my car.

Now I'm going to have to dump it.

"Yes. I know that's her vehicle," he said. "We have it on video. That's how we found her."

Video?

"Well, you better hurry up if'n you aim to catch her."

"Why is that ma'am?" he asked.

"She paid up her bill right before you showed up. I think she's getting ready to make a run for it."

Oh, she was so right about that.

I couldn't listen anymore. I had to get out of there. But I wasn't sure if I should head for the car – the one they had on video – or just start running.

I saw a dumpster.

I could jump into it and hide.

I looked down at myself. I had on jeans, a navy Polo jacket with a white shell underneath and tennis shoes.

Definitely dumpster-diving clothes.

I put my knapsack on the ground and took off my jacket. Using the sleeves, I tied it around my waist. Then I took the ponytail holder off my wrist and pulled my long hair back, looping it around. I needed to be aerodynamically poised to make my get away as fast as possible.

I was just going to run for it. Head to the car I decided. He didn't know what I looked like. Just that I was black. He wouldn't know it was me until I got into my car.

I stepped off the sidewalk onto the asphalt of the blacktop parking lot. I was sure I could make it to my car before he noticed me. I kept my eyes on my Jeep.

Why did I park so far?

I twisted my neck slightly to the left and from the corner of my eye, I saw FBI guy come out of the office door. He headed right, toward the room I had just vacated.

I picked up my pace.

Not much farther. I can do this.

I *can* do this.

I turned my neck to the right, looked over my shoulder, and just then his gaze caught mine.

Crap.

"Logan Dickerson," he shouted.

I started running.

Maybe he'll think I'm hard of hearing.

Trying to break into federally-guarded lands had been a bad idea, just as my mother warned. But who was she to talk? She had probably broken all kinds of laws and been involved with federal cover-ups and murders over the past few years.

I looked over my shoulder and there was FBI guy gaining on me. Yep. My mother was certainly no shining example and, to be honest, it was probably her fault that I turned out to have these criminal proclivities. Bad parenting.

"Hey! Stop!"

I ran toward my car, my luggage hitting every bump and hole, turning over off its wheels. Fumbling, I pointed the clicker and unlocked the door. I grabbed the handle and turned to see that he'd practically caught up with me.

Crap. Crap. Crap.

Before I could get my door open I felt his hand on my arm. Even though I knew he was there, it startled me and I jumped.

"Hey. Didn't you hear me calling you? he asked.

I was breathing hard. He didn't even seem winded. "No," I lied. My legs felt like they were going to buckle. I leaned up against the car.

"You didn't hear me?" He had an amused look on his face.

"Well," I started to stumble over my words. "I-I did . . . Sort of . . . I guess. I mean. I did." I swallowed hard. "But I didn't know who you were . . ."

Yeah, I'll go with that . . .

"You frightened me," I said with some mustered up bravado.

He reached in his back pocket.

Lord, was he going for handcuffs?

I knew this was it for me.

Chapter Three

"Where are you headed?" he asked. "He" was tall, with honey-colored skin. Dressed in a blue suit, white shirt and paisley tie, it was easy to notice the fit, firm body underneath that filled out his clothes.

"When?" I asked.

"Now. You seemed in such a hurry."

"I told you, you scared me." I licked my lips. "That's why I started running."

He looked at me and took in a breath.

"Sorry about that. Okay? I just was trying to get your attention." He bit his bottom lip and stared at me for a moment. "I'm with the FBI." He flashed me the badge he had pulled out of his pocket. "I just needed to ask you a couple of questions."

Whew! No handcuffs.

"FBI?" I pretended I hadn't known.

"Yes," he said.

"Oh, okay then." Now I acted like I was much calmer. I really wasn't. I was, in fact, more nervous than I'd been the night before when I was doing the actual crime.

Suddenly, I had to pee.

"So where are you headed?" he asked again.

"Stallings Island." The place just popped into my brain and I let it out.

A half-smile crept across his face. "Really?" He reached into his inside jacket pocket and pulled out a small notebook and pen.

"Yes." I stumbled forth with my lie. "It is an archaeological site in the coastal region of Georgia." I tried to speak more casually. "I'm an archaeologist. I'm doing research on the people that lived there approximately 4000 rcybp. R-C-Y-B-P. That's radio carbon years before present," I said in my most professional voice.

Figured I'd throw a little *sciencey* stuff in, maybe I'd sound less like a criminal.

"What kind of archaeologist are you, Ms. Dickerson?"

"It's *Doctor* Dickerson." I squared my shoulders and tried to stand up straighter. I had a Ph.D. in Anthropology *and* History, hopefully it would make me seem more like a law-abiding citizen. And flaunting it might help me appear more unfettered.

Although, I still had to put my hands behind my back because I couldn't seem to control them from trembling. My mouth wasn't having a hard time spilling lies, but the rest of my body seemed to rebel against it.

"My mother is a *biblical* archaeologist," I said.

Why did I say that?

I licked my lips again and shook my head. "And I-I'm just the run-of-the-mill, garden-variety type. Why?"

He wrote down something in his notebook. I tried to stand on my toes to see what it was.

"If you don't have any other questions," I said and adjusted my knapsack on my shoulder. "I was just getting ready to leave."

"There was a break-in at Track Rock Gap last night," he said, and looked up at me from his notebook. "Do you know anything about it?"

"Track Gap?" I said, trying to appear confused.

"Track Rock Gap," he corrected. "Don't tell me you haven't heard of it?"

Should I lie? I already had so many lies that I'd had to keep up with.

"Yes. I've heard of it." I decided on the truth. "Why?"

"Because your car was reported being seen there yesterday."

A knot rose in my throat.

Oh my God, I really am going to jail.

"We pulled it up on the security cam." He looked down at his notebook and flipped through a couple of pages.

"Ohio FYE 2965. That's your license plate?" He looked past me at my car.

"Yes," I said hesitantly.

"It was recorded around three o'clock yesterday. It shows you outside the gates . . ."

How could I be so stupid and not realize the place had surveillance cameras.

"Wait!" I blurted out. Suddenly it hit me. I felt a smile coming on. "My car was spotted at three o'clock?"

"Yes and -"

"In the afternoon?"

"Yes."

He's wasn't talking about when I was there last night.

He didn't know. He didn't know about last night.

I breathed in and exhaled a sigh of relief.

"Oh yes. I was there." My words flowed. "Thought I'd take a look at it, but it was locked up tight. No visitors I understand?" I raised my eyebrows.

"No. No one's allowed on the land. We were wondering did you see anyone else there. Or do you have any idea who was there last night?"

"No." I took in a breath. "No. I have no idea." I ran my hand over my face. "Okay, then. Is that all?"

"Just one more question."

"Alright," I said even though that was not how I felt.

"Where were you last night?" He looked me directly in my eyes.

Crap, I thought. *Can he tell if I lie? Had he been trained at Quantico to detect liars?*

"I don't know," I decided to lie anyway. "Sleep I guess."

"You don't know where you were?" He arched an eyebrow.

"Your question is kind of vague. Last night encompasses a lot of time," I said. "Do you mean after six? After nine?"

"After nine."

"In bed. Asleep," I said and nodded, lips tight.

"Are you sure?"

"I'm positive," I said. "I have no reason to lie."

Ha! If he only knew.

"I only ask because the woman at the desk -" He turned and looked back toward the motel, "said she saw you come in covered in dirt."

I frowned. "Yeah. I don't think that happened." Then I looked directly into his eyes. "Why would she say something like that?"

He kept his eyes locked on mine. A smirk appeared on his face. For some reason, that smirk made me nervous.

"I don't know why she would say that," he said finally. "Okay, well, if you remember seeing anything or anyone at Track Rock Gap while you were there, give me a call." He closed his notebook, then reached into the same inside jacket pocket and pulled out a business card. He handed it to me. "We're just trying to figure out if the person who broke in last night had come by earlier as well."

"I sure will." I held up the card. "I'll call if I think of anything," I said. I opened the back door and threw my luggage inside. I slammed that door, turned, smiled at him, and jumped in the driver's side. I took the satchel from around my neck, pushed the card he'd given me down in an inside pocket and threw it on the passenger seat. Then I pulled out of that parking lot so fast that I think I left tire marks.

I glanced back over at the parking lot before I turned the corner and saw that FBI man still standing there.

Dummy.

Yeah, I called you dummy.

I started grinning. "I got out of that one," I said aloud. "And he's none the wiser. Some kind of detective he is."

I drove over the bridge to the Interstate. I was going back home to Ohio. Do something nice for my mother. I turned on the car's GPS and Track Rock Gap popped up on the screen.

I glanced at myself in the rearview mirror, my light-brown skin glistening from my attempt at escape, and I thought about what I had done. The grin started to fade.

I really was turning into a criminal. Breaking onto government property, lying to FBI agents, and then feeling good about it. That suddenly made me feel terrible.

A remorseful criminal. *Geesh.*

I picked up my cell phone and punched in my mother's number. I was ready to admit I needed her help.

Chapter Four

I decided that I should actually go to Stallings Island.

I realized that I didn't want that FBI guy to check up on me and I wasn't where I said I'd be. I didn't want him to know how big a liar I turned out to be.

My mother would know how to make me be on Stallings Island – legally – happen. She'd know about any excavations there and how I could join a team.

When I got her on the phone, my mother, Dr. Justin Dickerson, famous, or in some circles, infamous, biblical archaeologist told me that Stallings Island was, much like Track Rock Gap, ran by a federal agency. And, she enlightened me, traffic to the island had in fact been shut down long ago to the public due to looting.

"Criminals," she had said and sucked her teeth. "I never could understand why people would break into places like that and desecrate our history."

If she only knew that her baby child had become one of those "people."

I decided to come clean with her. I had to tell her what I did in order to get her to use all of her clout to get me on the island so that my credibility in the science world wouldn't be shot.

Only I wasn't sure how much clout she had anymore.

My mother had discovered, way back in 1997, that hidden with the Dead Sea Scrolls were manuscripts that described an alternative history to man's origins. The manuscripts said that man – people just like us, same DNA, as she liked to say – had originated on Mars.

Yeah, right. It made my mother seem kind of wacky.

Unfortunately, before she could make it known to the general public, people that did know started getting killed over it, and secret societies that had government ties were trying to take the information from her. So she decided the world wasn't ready for what she knew.

Big decision for her to make, I know. But my mother is smart. Super smart. And if she thought it was best, well then so did I. So our family – including me – helped her hide all the evidence.

"One day," she had said, "this information will be rediscovered and the world will be ready to accept it for what it is and put it to good use."

She was good at cover-ups.

That was another reason I called her.

So my mother, after hearing my story and fussing at me for a good ten minutes about my impertinent and cheeky behavior and total disregard for the law, said she could probably get me permission to go to the island through her contacts with the Archaeological Conservancy, the agency now in charge of it.

Yay! She still had clout.

But, she cautioned, she didn't have the faintest idea how I was going to fake an excavation. She was sure that excavations, real or fake, weren't allowed. But she also said she'd keep trying to get me permission.

Maybe I could learn to listen a little bit more to my mother *before* heading out and trying to do things on my own.

She told me that Stallings Island was about eight miles outside of Augusta. And to try and be safe and truthful from here on out.

I promised I would.

I punched in Augusta on my GPS and headed south down the Georgia coastline. I opened up the window and let the breeze off the Savannah River flow through me. I turned up Maroon 5's *Sugar*, and enjoyed the drive.

Just off the highway to my left I watched seagulls fly over the sandy dunes, bluffs and windswept sea oats that led to the blue water and barrier islands. Shallow pools riffled where scores of fish, mussels, and shrimp swam.

And to my right sprawling live oaks and towering cypress trees glistening under the bright yellow sun seemed to sway with the beat of the music. The skies were a clear, heavenly blue. I took in a breath and smelled the fresh air. A grin curled up the side of my lips.

Yes. This was going to work out fine.

I could just feel it.

Chapter Five

Thursday Afternoon, BGD

There was no boat from Augusta to Stallings Island. No ferry. No bridge. No nothing.

No one was allowed on the island, so no one provided a way to get there. There was, I was told, a shoal – a sandbank – that extended from the shore to the Island. From what I understood, I could just walk across it.

When I asked for directions to the shoal, I was told it was in Yasamee, a small – no, very small – town just down the road "a piece." "A piece" turned out to be twenty-five miles. Augusta and Stallings Island were only eight miles apart *down* the river, but they were twenty-fives miles apart *over* land.

I found my way to Yasamee easy enough. The town was built around a square. The center a wide green open space with park benches and a gazebo, and its four sides were anchored with a movie theater, barber shop, diner and a library. I stopped at one end of it and scanned over each building looking for a hotel. Nothing.

I drove down the streets that dead ended at the square and found all of them lined with beautiful water hickory and tupelo trees and filled with vibrantly painted houses of Eastlake and Italianate styled architecture. It was like driving through the streets of a picture. I drove along the coast and saw a beautiful beachfront property. But there was no hotel in sight.

Then I spotted it – a quaint bed and breakfast, just like the ones in travel magazines, on one of the last streets I drove down. The sign outside read "Maypop B & B." Maypop was the edible fruit of the North American passion flower.

"Perfect," I whispered.

From the outside the house looked enormous. It was white with black shutters framing an abundance of front windows. It had double oak doors and a wrap-around porch on both the first and second story. I found a place to park right outside the house. After grabbing my knapsack, I strolled up the brick walkway past the verdant, perfectly manicured green lawn and pink azalea bushes, up the steps and onto the porch.

The tan, natural coir doormat read "Welcome" in big, bold black letters and that was just how I felt.

Chapter Six

Thursday Around Suppertime, BGD

A bell, fitted to the top of the double oak doors, tinkled as I came in. I walked into a large foyer, its walls painted a rich cranberry ended at glossy, polished wood floors where a large round plush, patterned rug sat in its center. There was an oak staircase, and to the left of it an ornately carved wooden counter that blocked the entrance to a hallway that led to the back of the house. Off to the side was a large dining area that was filled with people.

The smell of something hot and sweet stopped me in my tracks.

What in the world is that?

Taking in the aroma, I turned toward the dining room and saw that everyone in there was looking at me.

"Hi." A woman wended her way around tables and came to me with her hand stuck out. "I'm Renmar Colquett. Welcome to the Maypop." She had a big, genuine smile on her face.

"Hi." I said. "I'm Logan. Logan Dickerson. I wanted to get a room?"

"Oh that's wonderful," she said her eyes beaming. "Well, come on, let's get you checked in. She looked over her shoulder, back into the dining area. "Brie, we have a guest."

The person she called Brie came over and clapped her palms together. "Oh my. How nice," she said, her smile just as big as Renmar's.

"Her name's Logan Dickerson," Renmar said to Brie, then to me, "This is my sister, Brie Pennywell," Renmar pointed to Brie, "and," Renmar twisted her body from the waist to look around her. "Mother," she called out, and "Mother" came from the hallway that was behind the counter, carrying a purse on her arm, and a wheaten Scottish terrier following behind her.

"And this is our mother, Vivienne Pennywell and her dog, Cat." Renmar said. "But everyone calls her Miss Vivee." Renmar looked at her mother and the dog. "My mother that is. Not the dog. Everybody calls my mother, Miss Vivee." She placed her hand on her mother's shoulder and then turned back to the dining room.

"And that's Hazel Cobb," she said pointing. "My oldest and dearest friend."

Hazel was walking toward me when Renmar started the introduction. The only black person I'd seen since I arrived, she wrapped her arms around me. "I'm a hugger," she said. "I hope you don't mind."

"And then everyone else," Renmar said and swept her arm out toward the dining room. "Well. Everyone that's here today at least. But if you stay long enough you'll meet everyone because everybody from town comes here at least once a week to eat."

When she introduced me to "everyone" the majority of them got up and came out into the foyer. They shook my hand, patted me on my back, and introduced themselves, their wives, husbands, and children to me. I'm sure I'd never remember who was who.

But man, wasn't this just the friendliest place?

Renmar, the apparent proprietor, reminded me of a southern belle. Sophisticated, sleek, she looked to be in her late-fifties. She had on a sleeveless sheath burgundy dress, burgundy two inch heels that were made from Plexiglas or something transparent resembling glass. She was classy. She had her brown hair cut into a stylish bob and her make-up made her skin look like that of a porcelain doll.

Brie on the other hand looked motherly. She wore her light brown hair in a French roll, and had a sprinkle of freckles that ran across her nose. She was slightly overweight, wore a loosely-stitched crocheted cardigan over her belted, cotton green dress and low heeled loafers.

"Mother" was old. Old like ninety-odd-something old. But seemed spry. She walked without a cane, or walker. She was slender and short – like five-foot nothing short. She had on a thin, off-white coat with a big round collar. Her hair was long, mostly white, but there were sparse strands of black mixed in. It was braided in the back had been brought over her shoulder to rest on her chest. Loose wisps framed her face. She eyed me from the time she came out for her introduction. I couldn't tell from her expression what she was thinking and, unlike everyone else, she didn't say a word to me.

"We don't get many guests," Renmar said pulling a guest register from underneath the counter. "Ever since they banned tourists from going to the Island no one comes to visit Yasamee anymore."

"What ya doing down here in these parts." It was Brie that spoke.

"I'm an archaeologist," I said, which made everyone quiet down and look at me. "I'm here to work over on Stallings Island." It wasn't a complete lie. That is if my mother came through for me. I was going to act the part though, even if I had lost the trail of that stupid FBI guy. I still had to do my penance.

"You have permission to dig on the Island?" Renmar asked me but she was looking at the man who had wandered in during the introductions. He had a pretty blonde woman on his arm, both puffed on an e-cigarette and were very much into – it appeared – public displays of affection.

"Yes. Well, sort of. Why?" I asked and let me eyes dart from Renmar to the man. I hoped they didn't know something I didn't know and I would be made out to be a liar once again.

"No reason," she said and lowered her eyes.

"Wait," Brie said, her eyes seemed to light up. "What's your last name?"

"Dickerson."

"And you're an archaeologist?"

"Yes."

"Oh it couldn't be." She clapped her hand again and cocked her head.

She was making me nervous. Had she heard about me and Track Rock Gap? I heard gossip travelled fast in small towns.

Although me being at Track Rock Gap wasn't exactly gossip. It was true.

"Are you related to the biblical archaeologist, Justin Dickerson?" she asked.

"Yes, I am," I said warily. I never knew what people were going to say when they mentioned my mother. "She's my mother."

That made Brie scream.

"Oh my goodness," she said. "Her mother wrote a book."

Oh. No.

"My mother and I -"

But before I could stop her she blurted it out.

"The book is proof that we all came from Mars."

I took in a deep breath.

Everyone got quiet. They seemed to be holding their breath. The silence was nauseating.

"Brie!" Renmar said. "Don't be ridiculous." Renmar looked at me apologetically. "Brie gets carried away sometimes. I'm sure she's got it all confused."

"Yes," I said and smiled.

There was a collective exhale in the room.

"Noooo." Brie's eyes got even bigger. "I don't think so. I'm pretty sure I'm right about this."

Technically Brie was right. My mother had written a book about what she discovered. Two books to be exact, and the first one, the only one Brie could have read was written as fiction. But that's another story.

Fortunately no one was paying any attention to her. Except the little old lady. Miss Vivee. I saw a smile creep across her face right before she turned and walked back down the hallway with her dog, Cat.

"Rooms are thirty-nine dollars a night and we serve breakfast and dessert here." Renmar's words got my attention. "For your other meals, you can either go into the kitchen," she pointed in the direction with a tilt of her head, "and grab yourself something or go to Jellybean Café up in the town square."

"Yes," I said. "I think I saw it coming in."

"Viola Rose will take good care of you," Renmar said. "She thinks that her husband, Gus, is almost as good a cook as I am."

That elicited an uproar of laughter. I felt myself smiling just because everyone around me was so happy.

"You want some dessert?" Brie asked. She didn't say anything else about my mother, but I could tell she wasn't through with me.

"Sure," I said. Not letting her suspicions (rather the truth) about my mother affect how this town and crowd made me feel.

"Well, come on then," Renmar said, and ushered me into the dining room. "Brie, get her some pie. A great big piece of pie." She looked at me. "Do you drink coffee?"

"Yes."

"And a cup of coffee, too," she yelled after Brie.

Brie came back with a slice of blueberry pie, a fork and napkin, and a hot cup of black coffee. She sat it all in front of me and smiled in anticipation.

"Enjoy," Renmar said, then turned around and shooed everyone away. "Let her enjoy her pie."

I smiled and as I cut into it with my fork. Steam rose through the crisscrossed layers of the flaky crust and the rich, royal blue of the berries over-stuffed inside oozed out.

I lifted the fork up to my mouth and let my lips wrap around the big chunk that I'd cut off. I slid it into my mouth and savored the explosion of sweet, gooey, goodness as my tongue turned it over.

Oh. My. What could be better than this?

Chapter Seven

Friday Morning

I got up early the next morning. My mother had gotten me an in, so I thought it best that I go over to the Island and check it out. I had to make good on all my lies and put the Track Rock Gap debacle behind me.

As I came down the steps a waft of freshly-baked bread beckoned me to the kitchen. I peeked into the dining area and saw people eating and talking at the many tables while Brie acted as server, smiling and chatting at every table she passed.

There was that one couple from last night, I noted. Heads together, so in love. The guy Renmar eyed when I said I was going to Stallings Island. I didn't recognize any of the other people, but everyone seemed to know one another. Meals around here seemed more like a small get together of friends and family.

Wait. I stopped to get a better look at the couple from last night. I did recognize the man from the night before, he was still puffing on an e-cigarette. But that wasn't the same woman. I was sure of it. He was with *another* woman. *Oh my.* I giggled. *Cheating in public like that.* He's gonna get himself shot.

I wandered into the huge chef's kitchen. Wall to wall bright white cabinets, aluminum appliances – a six burner gas stove with a built-in griddle, and a bottom-freezer, side-by-side-refrigerator met me. A rust and black checkerboard cork floor, a large farmhouse sink, with a shiny silver backsplash behind it and a moss, beige and rust colored rug that sat below it, complimented the green moss colored walls. Renmar stood on the other side of an oversized island with a butcher block top.

"What's your story, morning glory?" Renmar asked glancing up at me. She was up to her elbows in flour.

"Pardon me?"

"You're up early. Whatch'ya up to?"

"Oh. Yeah," I said and smiled. "I'm an early riser." I sat down on a kitchen stool. "Thought I'd go over to Stallings Island. Check it out. See what I'm getting myself into." I leaned in to see what she was doing. "What're you making?"

"Biscuits. And you're just in time for some hot ones." She glanced over at the oven. "They're almost ready."

"Sounds good." My mouth was starting to water.

"Have you spoken to Oliver Gibbons?" she asked as she floured her rolling pin.

"I don't know who he is."

"You know, the gentlemen that always has a lady on his arm." She looked up at me and winked.

"Oh. Yes. I do know who he is."

The cheater.

"I saw him out in the dining room before I came in here to see what smelled so good. Does he know anything about the Island?"

"He knows *everything* about the Island. He lives right by the shoal. Beautiful beach house."

"I think I saw the house yesterday when I drove in." I nodded remembering the gray cottage surrounded by sand, sea oats and morning glories. "Does he know anything about the history of it?"

"Everyone here knows the history of the Island," she said. She pulled the tea towel off her shoulder and wiped her hands. Reaching in the refrigerator, she grabbed a small ramekin with a handle. She handed it to me with a spoon.

"What's this?"

"A little fruit. Grapefruit, oranges, blueberries. Strawberries."

"So I don't know if I should ask Mr. Gibbons." I took a mouthful of the fruit. "I don't really know him. I wouldn't want to impose."

"It's Oliver. Just call him Oliver. Nobody around here is much on formalities. And he won't mind a bit. In fact, I already spoke to him about you. He'll be happy to help you."

"Mmmm. This is delicious," I said, chucking in another juicy spoonful. "What's in this?" I gave her a questioning look. "It isn't just fruit juices?"

A half-smile crossed her lips. "No. It isn't," she said proudly.

"What else you put in here?"

"Now. If I told ya that," she wiped her hands on her frilly pink apron. "I'd have to kill ya," she said cocking her head to the side with a smile that I wasn't quite sure if it was genuine or not.

She went over to the stainless steel double oven. "Perfect," she said as she pulled a rack of lightly browned biscuits.

"Those look good." I raked the last of the fruit from the small bowl into my mouth. I wanted to stick my tongue in it and lick it clean. But, I remembered my manners. "Are you serving those for breakfast?" I nodded toward the biscuits.

"I sure am," she said and saw me staring at the biscuits. "Why don't you go on out to the dining room and find yourself a seat," Renmar said and nodded with her head toward the front of the house. "I'll bring you out a couple of these and you can check out the menu to see what else you want for breakfast." She laid the rack of biscuits on the end of the butcher block island.

"Here," she said with her southern drawl. "Take another cuppa' fruit with you." She pulled out a tray of the ramekins from the side-by-side, sat them on the table and handed me one. "And don't tell nobody I gave you two." She pointed a finger at me. "When folks ask for seconds I tell them, 'No.' They're so popular I have to ration them out."

"I can see why," I said coveting the one she handed me.

"Now go on. Get!" She turned me around by my shoulders and gave me a gentle push. "Brie'll take your order," she said. I turned and smiled at her as she started brushing butter on the tops of the biscuits. "And I'll bring you some of these," she called after me.

I held on tight to my cup of fruit and found a table in the far corner of the room near the front of the house. I looked over and saw Oliver Gibbons, cigarette hanging from his lips, right where I had spotted him earlier.

Such a flirt.

Leaning in close, whispering to her, "Casanova" Gibbons touched his woman companion tenderly. He hovered over her as if she was his one and only and he was madly in love with her. Yet, she clearly was a different blonde than the one I saw him with the day before. The one he had treated the same way as he was now treating this woman.

I chuckled as I watched him. In such a small town, how could he get away with what he was doing?

And why did Renmar talk to him about me? I wonder what she could have said.

I couldn't do any real work over at the Island until my mother got back with me. I pulled out my phone and checked to see if I had missed any calls or texts from her. I didn't want to get jammed up in a bunch of lies with these people here like I had done with FBI Guy. They were such nice people.

Looking up from my phone, I saw Brie taking an order at a table across the room. I waved her over and she held up a finger. "Be right witc'ya, Honeybun," she said and smiled. "You want me to bring some coffee?"

I nodded. The two cups of fruit were filling, but I figured I'd still order something to go with the biscuits that Renmar was bringing out for me.

I looked back down at my phone. No missed calls. No texts. Figuring I'd check the weather while I waited for Brie, I tapped on Safari and typed in *www.weather.com*. Lifting my eyes from the phone, I saw Brie go over and start to pick up a pot of coffee from the warmer, but someone coming in the front door distracted her from refilling any cups.

Nearly dropping the glass pot, she ran to the door on the other side of the wall from where I sat. Once she went behind the wall I couldn't see her, but I could hear her clearly.

Everyone could hear her.

"Bay!" I heard her exclaim. "I can't believe ya' here! Boy, com'ere. Give me a hug. Ain't you a sight for sore eyes?"

Then she appeared from behind the wall, back in the doorway, pulling someone behind her. She called toward the kitchen. "Renmar!" she yelled. "Come here right now! You ain't gone believe who's here." And then *he* walked into my line of sight.

I dropped my phone into the ramekin in front of me.

Oh crap!

I slid down in my seat. I wanted to crawl under the table.

It was the FBI guy from Itza.

Had he followed me here?

Was he here to arrest me?

Brie sure seemed to know him. But it seemed that everyone around here knew everyone else, so that might not mean too much.

"Bay!" This time it was Renmar who screamed his name. She ran out from the back and practically threw herself against him and wrapped him in a bear hug.

"Hi, Ma," he said.

She's his mother? Jesus!

"My baby." Renmar pushed away from him and gave him a once over, then she grabbed him and hugged him tight. Again. Over her shoulder, she must've spotted Miss Vivee. "Mother," she said breaking her hold on FBI Guy. "Look what the cat drug in!"

"Grandmother," Bay said turning to Miss Vivee just as she came into my sight. "Look at you. You look younger every time I see you."

She put her arm out to him, a big grin on her face. "There's my baby."

And then everyone in the dining room got up to see him. Smiling. Kissing him. Shaking his hand. It was like a movie star had just graced their presence.

"Bay Colquett." Loverboy Oliver Gibbons joined the chorus. "It's good to see you," he said shaking his hand

Not for me. I had hoped to never see this man again.

I dug in my satchel and pulled out the business card he'd given me.

Bay Colquett.

Sure enough, that was what was written on the front of it. He never told me his name. Just announced "FBI" and pushed his stupid badge in my face. When he was finished interrogating me, he gave me the card and instead of looking at it, I just shoved it down in my purse.

I should have read it.

Because if I had, as soon as Renmar told me her last name, whether I thought they were related or not, I would have turned and bolted for the door. Down the steps two at a time.

I took my phone out of the fruit bowl and dried it as best I could, then wrapped it in one of the cloth napkins.

I had to get out without him seeing me.

I put my knapsack over my head and adjusted it on my shoulder. I slid out of the chair and looked over to the door that led to the kitchen. Only about twenty-five feet . . . If I could just get across the dining room without too much noise . . . I just might make it through the kitchen and out the back door without him seeing me.

I crept across the room, berating myself for sitting so far to the front of it. I kept a watchful eye on the crowd surrounding FBI Guy.

That's right, everyone, keep him occupied.

Only a few more steps, I turned my head and looked at the door. Just a couple -

"Dr. Dickerson."

I knew that voice.

Crap.

I turned and looked out to the foyer where everyone was now looking at me.

And there he was with that stupid smirk.

"I thought that was your car outside," he said. "I see you made it. Get much excavating done yet?"

I should have not worried about covering up my lies and gone home to my mother.

Chapter Eight

Friday Afternoon

It didn't smell like the mouthwatering pastry that I smelled the first evening I'd set foot in the Maypop Bed & Breakfast. It smelled fishy even before I got in the door. People were milling around outside, whispering among themselves and watching the house.

I had spent the morning getting a new phone. Renmar's juicy secret recipe didn't go well with the wiring of an iPhone 6.

I had planned on spending the morning on the Island but that FBI guy – Bay Colquett – showing up had got me so flustered. I drove out to Augusta because, of course, there was no mobile phone store in Yasamee. On my way back I stopped at the Stallings Inn. It was, I found, the only other sleeping accommodation in town. It was quiet and empty. +

My mother was working on people to get me approved to do some work on the Island and I couldn't just leave now that she'd gotten other people involved. My phony cover-up story was causing more trouble than I bargained for. Until I heard back from my mother, I decided that I was moving out of the Maypop Bed & Breakfast and away from Bay Colquett. Stallings Inn would work just fine.

But once I got inside, everything changed. And things looked even fishier than they had from the outside.

The place was overflowing with people. The Sheriff was shouting at people, Renmar was crying, eyes red and puffy, and the lady I remembered as Hazel Cobb was trying to comfort her. It was bedlam. And then I spotted, Vivienne Pennywell, sitting quietly there in midst of it.

Miss Vivee sat on the light beige, tufted armed bench in the corner of the foyer. She had on a sun hat and sunglasses, a thin, powder blue coat with a large rounded collar, and knee-high rubber boots. Her dog sat on her lap.

She pulled her sunglasses down on her nose and beckoned me with her finger. She mouthed "Come here," then patted the seat next to her.

I snaked my way through the crowd and sat where she had directed. "What happened?" I asked.

"Gemma Burke died, face down, in her bowl of bouillabaisse."

"Here?"

"Sitting right there in the dining room."

I followed the bony, shaky finger as she pointed over to a lone bowl sitting on a table in the middle of the room.

"She bounced in, ponytail keeping pace swinging from side-to-side, full of life. Left cold and stiff in a black bag."

"That's terrible," I said "Was she young?"

"Round about your age."

"I don't think I met her," I said, trying to place the name with a face.

"You didn't. She had come in for lunch."

"I thought you only served breakfast and dessert here." I frowned.

"Not on Fridays. On Fridays we serve breakfast, dessert, and lunch."

"Do you ever serve dinner?"

"No."

"Well, where is that FBI guy?" I peered around through the crowd, hoping he wasn't still around.

"You don't know much about the law, do you, Missy?"

"I'm . . . Logan," I said placing my hand on my chest. "Remember?"

"I know your name. I'm just saying the FBI wouldn't be in charge of something like this unless it happened on federal property. You know places like banks, national parks or federally-owned land." She eyed me curiously and then pushed her glasses back up her nose.

"I didn't mean that."

Really, what I wanted to know was if he had been looking for me. I was nervous about any videotape recording being found that showed me running around Track Rock Gap like a lunatic. But I couldn't let her know that.

"I was just asking," I said and changed the subject. "So Renmar must have known this Gemma well. She seems pretty upset."

"No. Not really." Her nonchalant expression never changed. "Gemma used to live here in Yasamee when she was growing up and then she moved away. Just came back recently. Can't say that Renmar knew much of her, other than that girl loved her bouillabaisse."

"Then why is she crying?" I watched as Hazel Cobb nestled Renmar on her shoulder and stroked her head. She was sniffling and saying something indecipherable between sobs.

"Gemma Burke died while eating her fish stew. Stands to reason she'd be upset. Everyone is going to think that Renmar's dish must've poisoned her." She pulled her sunglasses down on her nose again. "Don't you see all these people? In the house? All along the walkway out front? Probably the whole town has come out. Renmar's worried. She doesn't want word to get around that her famous bouillabaisse is lethal."

I nodded and made a mental note not to eat anything else out of Renmar's kitchen. Too bad, because she made the best food I'd ever eaten.

"She wasn't poisoned though," Miss Vivee said matter-of-factly.

"How do you know?"

"I know Renmar's bouillabaisse."

"Maybe the girl had a heart attack or something?" I suggested.

"Good Lord, no," Miss Vivee said, keeping her eyes trained on all the goings on. "Although the way she was always out running like somebody was chasing her, dressed in those stretchy clothes, I'm surprised that her heart didn't burst open from all the exercise."

"She jogged?"

No answer from Miss Vivee, just a look that asked if I were slow.

"You don't think jogging is good for you?" I asked. Thought I'd try a different approach.

"If people were supposed to go around running for miles, God would've put them on that speed from the word go. No one has any business moving that fast. For nothing."

I laughed. "I'm with you on that."

Miss Vivee lowered her voice. "Gemma Burke's death wasn't natural. I can assure you of that."

"You don't think so?"

"I know so," she said and stroked her dog's head. "That girl was murdered."

"Oh my." A chill ran up my spine. "That would be terrible if it were true."

"It is true." She pushed Cat off her lap, took off her sunglasses, and turned to me. Her whole expression changed. "Oh, but you missed all the hullabaloo." She was suddenly animated, her eyes sparkling. "Coroner came, zipped Gemma Burke in his death bag and hauled her away on a gurney. No pomp. No circumstance. Zip and done.

"Sheriff Haynes and the deputy got here when they were wheeling the body out. Been asking questions ever since." She nodded to the pandemonium in the foyer.

"What's the deputy's name?" I asked. He looked about my age, nice looking, but seemed lost in all the commotion. He was nursing a hand that was bandaged and people kept bumping into it. It was making him even more agitated.

"Colin Pritchard," Miss Vivee said. "Born and bred here in Yasamee, but he went and did his Peace Officer training up north." She glanced over at me. "You'd never know he had any training in anything."

I chuckled. I guess it was pretty obvious he didn't know what he was doing.

"But Lloyd Haynes, the sheriff-" she nodded in his direction, "ain't had no training, and probably never been at the scene of a crime like this before. But he looks pretty darn competent, don't he?"

I nodded. "Look like he's got a hurt foot?"

"Yep," Miss Vivee said. "He and that deputy of his always out fishing and hunting." She pointed to the Deputy's hand. "They do more damage to themselves than to whatever they're hunting."

I laughed. "And those are the two that's licensed to protect around here?"

"It's a sad story, I know," she said. "Anyway. Sorry you missed it. Bet you would have enjoyed it. Seeing Gemma Burke like that," she said and nodded toward the dining hall, as if Gemma Burke was still there. "Face purple, her eyes open and lifeless. A real sight to see." She looked at me. "You like dead things, right?"

Chapter Nine

An hour later, the chaos hadn't stopped.

Miss Vivee and I stayed seated on the bench and watched as the first murder in Yasamee in the last sixty-five years was investigated.

Sheriff Lloyd Haynes and Deputy Colin Pritchard spent the morning talking to all the people that had been at the Maypop when Gemma died. Now the Sheriff was trying to get Renmar's account of the events.

"Oh my," Renmar said, her tears still flowing after sixty whole minutes. "I don't know what to say." She looked at Hazel Cobb who was holding on to her, then she lowered her eyes and toyed with the tissue in her hand. "Gemma came in here every Friday since she got back. She was such a skinny little thing. All that exercise I guess. I was happy to feed her."

"She loved your bouillabaisse," Hazel said and nodded.

"Yes. She did," Renmar said and nodded back.

Sheriff Haynes pulled his brown, four-dented hat off of his head, and swiped his hand though the tuft of chestnut hair that fell in his face. Though he seemed hot and frustrated, he kept a cool temper. He was slightly tanned with dark brown eyes and a square jawline. He looked to be in his late fifties or early sixties, and his tan colored, short-sleeved uniform hung well over his fit body. But with all the disorder he was dealing with, it seemed Renmar's reaction to everything was giving him the most grief.

"And -" the Sheriff started to say something more to her when the deputy came up and interrupted his questioning. Deputy Pritchard leaned into him and spoke low and close to his ear. When he finished speaking to him, the Sheriff said, "Excuse me, Renmar, I'll be right back." He left out the front door following the deputy.

As soon as he left, Renmar sent Hazel upstairs for something and then pulled Oliver close to her. They spoke in hushed and hurried voices. Oliver puffed hard on his e-cigarette and squinted, taking in what Renmar was saying. Renmar's eyes flitted about the room as if she was ensuring no one was looking. We locked eyes momentarily. Then her eyes darted from me, to Miss Vivee and back before she turned again to Oliver.

I turned to Miss Vivee. "What they got their heads together about?" I asked.

"Your guess is as good as mine. Maybe they're trying to get their alibis together."

"You're enjoying this aren't you?"

"Why who wouldn't?" Miss Vivee said. "It's a real crime scene around here. They roped off everything with that yellow tape, stuffed things into small plastic bags, and took a boatload of pictures. Most excitement I've seen in forty years or more."

The Sheriff came back in and Renmar pushed Oliver toward the back of the house. He hurried off, furtively glancing back over his shoulder. Renmar tried to control her sniffles. Patting her hair and licking her lips, it was quite noticeable that she was trying to remain calm.

"I hate to tell you, Renmar." The Sheriff was back. "But we're going to have to take that bowl of bouillabaisse that Gemma was eating when she . . . Well, you know."

"When she croaked," Miss Vivee said in a voice that, it seemed, was loud as her little frame could muster.

"Yes. Well," the Sheriff said somewhat flustered.

"Kicked the bucket," Miss Vivee offered.

"Mother," Renmar said.

"Hah," Miss Vivee said. "I could do this all night. I've got a million of them," she yelled out. "Bite the dust. That's another one," she said laughing and elbowed me.

"Anyway," the Sheriff said, raising his voice. "I'm going to need the whole pot as well."

"It's all gone," Renmar said. And as soon as it came out of her mouth, Miss Vivee hit me on my thigh. I looked at her.

"That's a lie," she said out of the side of her mouth. "There's a whole eighteen-quart stockpot full of it on the stove."

"All gone?" The Sheriff hadn't heard Miss Vivee, but it seemed like he didn't believe Renmar either. "Mind if I take a look?"

"Help yourself," Renmar said, and swept her arm in the direction of the kitchen. "I gave the last bowl to Gemma." She set her lips firmly and locked eyes with the Sheriff.

He held her gaze momentarily, and then headed off to the kitchen without saying a word. Renmar followed behind him.

"They'll do an autopsy, no doubt," Miss Vivee said, looking out into the distance. "But if they think that Renmar's fish stew done Gemma Burke in, they'll soon learn that they're barking up the wrong tree. I told the Sheriff that, too. He just smiled and nodded his head. Patronizing son-of-a-gun. The facts will prove me right. Wait and see."

Miss Vivee got quiet, and then took in a breath and shook her head. "Her hair was a mess," she said, her voice a husky whisper. "Poor Gemma Burke. When they pulled her face up out the bowl it was just a mess. All wet around the edges from falling into the fish stew." She crunched up her nose. "When I go," she said with a nod of her head, her voice back to normal, "I plan on looking like I was just getting ready to sit for my sweet sixteen portrait. Rosy cheeks and all. Even if I have to apply a little rouge. And not a hair out of place. I'll make sure of that."

"Oh really?"

"Yes really," she said as if it were a fact. "I'm sure God'll give me the strength to make myself presentable when it's time for us to meet." Miss Vivee smiled and patted me on my knee.

I looked up to see Deputy Colin Pritchard standing over me. He smelled all woody and fresh, and I took in a big whiff. He was tall and he looked so buff and officious in his tan uniform. But his eyes and awkward smile made him look vulnerable, too. Especially with his hand wrapped in a bandage. I just wanted to kiss his "booboo" and make it feel better.

I wouldn't mind kissing those lips either.

"Yes," I said. My eyes met his. "You need me?"

"May I speak with you," he asked. "I need to talk to you about where you were this morning."

"Sure," I said. "I don't mind."

"Looks like you're a suspect, too," Miss Vivee said with a mischievous wink.

Chapter Ten

"I've decided to solve the murder."

Vivienne Pennywell made her announcement as she came out the house, followed by her dog, and sat next to me on the porch swing.

"You have?" I asked.

"I have." She set her lips in a firm line. She seemed quite resolute.

I didn't say anything at first, making sure she didn't have any more to add. I had just finished giving my statement to the deputy and thought I'd get away from all the fray that was still going on in the house. The crowd of people outside had nearly dissipated. After Miss Vivee's comment though, I realized I probably would've been better off staying inside.

I thought I'd try my "no murder happened" approach again.

"Maybe nothing happened," I said. "It is possible that she had an aneurysm or a heart attack or something. Something natural."

"I told you once, there wasn't anything natural about her death. I know exactly how she died, and I aim to find out what caused it." She paused and threw me a glance. "I might need help, though."

"You want me to help?" I pointed to myself and shook my head. "No. Not me," I said as I furrowed my brow.

"Yes you," she said. "Seems like you got a streak of mischief in you. Thinking you'd make a good partner."

"A streak of mischief? What makes you say that?" I shook my head. "Not me," I said again. "I'm as upstanding as you can get."

"That's not what I heard." The edges of her lips turned up in a grin.

That stupid FBI guy.

"What did you hear?" I asked. "I'm sure no one knows anything about me. I just got here."

"My grandson told me you thought you were Indiana Jones."

"Indiana Jones? He doesn't . . . I didn't . . . I don't know why he'd say that."

"Are you? You are an archaeologist. They're good at digging up stuff and piecing together clues."

"Am I like Indiana Jones? No. Not at all. How do you know who that is anyway?"

"When you get to be my age all you do is watch TV. It keeps people from thinking you've gone daft when they see you staring off into space 'cause your mind done gone blank. You stare at the TV, that way they think you're engrossed in a show."

"I'm not anything like Indiana Jones," I repeated and shook my head. "Nothing like that. Maybe my mother is," I added under my breath. "But not me."

"Sounds like your mother is a hoot," Miss Vivee said with a gleam in her eye. "Believing in Martians. You must have had a ball growing up." She smiled at me. "Maybe you think outside the box like she does? That's the kind of thinking you need to solve a murder, you know."

"That may be a little much for you," I said. "Solving a murder. Seeing that you're . . . older." I coughed into my hand. "I think that Sheriff Haynes and Deputy Pritchard just might have everything covered. Don't you?"

"Don't patronize me," she said. "If I thought they had everything covered, I wouldn't say I was going to solve it myself."

"And why don't you think they can handle it?"

"Lloyd Haynes is a good man, and eventually I think he may get to it, but by that time the Maypop

Bed & Breakfast will have a reputation of its food killing customers. Renmar's already in there bawling her eyes out on Hazel Cobb's shoulder. With the Maypop in ruin, there'd go me and my girls' livelihood and our good name. Just can't let that happen." She sucked her teeth. "And that Colin Pritchard, well he's about as dumb as a box of rocks."

I laughed. "He did seem like he was bumbling things at first," I said. "But after I talked to him he seemed pretty sharp to me. Took down all my information. Asked the right kind of questions."

And he was cute. Very cute. Nice body, and he had the most beautiful emerald green eyes I'd ever seen. And that dimple in his chin was just too sexy.

"He asked me where I was when Gemma Burke died," Miss Vivee's continued talking brought me back from my reverie. "How crazy is that? Now if that don't tell you the man don't know shit from Shinola shoe polish, I don't know what does."

"That sounds like a good question to me. He needs to check out everyone's alibi."

"Well, it's not a good question," she said with an air of disgust. "At least not a good one to ask me. Everyone in this town, all five hundred and eighty-three of 'em, know that I haven't left this house in twenty years. Nearly all his life. So where else would I be? Even Cat knew he was asking dumb questions.

She barked at him the entire time. That boy ain't got half a brain. He couldn't find his way out of a paper bag." She bit her bottom lip and scratched across her chin with her fingertip. "But I think I can find out what happened. Maybe even before the Sheriff does. I'm already one step ahead of him."

"How's that?"

"I know that Renmar's bouillabaisse didn't kill her." She paused. "And with the body having to be sent to Augusta for the autopsy, we'll have a least a week's jump on the Sheriff's investigation."

"Why do you want me to help you?"

"I just told you, you've got experience in digging up stuff. Plus, you think anyone else around here'll help me?"

No, I thought. *Because no else around here cares if you know they think you're crazy.*

"Do you really hail from Ohio?" she asked.

"I do." I nodded. "I'm from Cleveland. And before you ask, I don't think I'm from Mars. And neither does my mother."

"Too bad. That may have actually worked to our advantage." She looked at me. "Super powers and all."

"How did you know I was from Ohio?" I asked.

"Bay told me." She took in a breath. "I'm from Ohio, too. That's a secret, though. But since we gonna be partners, thought I should tell you that up front."

"I would've thought you were born in Georgia."

"That's just what I tell my girls. They don't need to know everything about me. I'm a hundred years old. I've done a lot of things in my time. But nobody around here is old enough to remember anything about me. I, on the other hand, remember pretty much everything about everybody."

"You're a hundred?" I wouldn't have ever thought she was that old. She got around really well, and was so alert.

Maybe I had been too stereotypical when assessing her.

"Closer to it than anybody else around here. But not too old to conduct a murder investigation." She nodded her head. "You can be sure of that."

"You have any experience solving murders?"

"Don't need any experience. Just common sense and I've got plenty of that. But like I said, I need a partner. Just not sure if I can trust you or not," she said.

"Understandable," I said, seeing the need to start trying to get out of this "partner" thing. "But-," I tried to look sympathetic, "I wouldn't have much time to help you with your sleuthing, anyway. I've got my own digging to do. I've got my work over on Stallings Island, remember?"

She cut her eyes over at me. "You and I both know that you don't have no real business over there."

"What? What do you mean?"

"And I'm just as sure that it was you that was snooping around up there by Gainesville. In that locked up government reservation."

I opened my mouth to say something.

"Don't lie," she said. "You know it's the truth. My grandson, Bay, is good at his job. He said he knows it was you, but they didn't have any proof."

Ugghh! I do not like that man.

"But no never mind 'cause that'll work out fine for us," she said. "I'll just tell everyone I'm helping you over at the Island." A smile came across her face, and she leaned in to me. "That could be our cover."

"Cover?"

"Yes. The story we'll tell everyone why, after all these years, I'm leaving the house. Why we're spending time together. Believe me, the people around here'll wonder. I'll just say you need me to help over at the Island."

I was all too familiar with cover stories. That was the reason I was in Yasamee in the first place.

"And what will you say I need you to help me do?" I asked.

"Dig, of course. Isn't that what you people do?"

"Are people going to believe that?"

"Probably not, but they're not going to call me a liar. Not to my face. More than likely, they'll just smile and nod their heads trying to pacify what they think is a crazy old woman. But no one will be able to prove I'm lying because no one is allowed to be on the Island. It's really perfect."

I arched an eyebrow. *Maybe they wouldn't be so far off thinking she was crazy.*

"I'll say I'm digging for Indian remains when really we'll be digging for clues."

I rolled my eyes.

"What about Oliver?" I decided to ask instead of voicing my opinion about the cover story she was making up. "He was supposed to be helping me," I said.

"I suspect we'll have to concoct a story about that, too." Miss Vivee glanced at me. "If push comes to shove, we might have to let him in on our little caper. We'll see how that goes. But for right now, mum's the word." She patted me on my knee. "Can't let on to folks what we're doing."

"Ooookay then." There seemed to be no wiggling out of this one. At least for now. Plus, I was sure, at her age, this little fantasy of hers wouldn't last long. "I'm in," I said. "Where should we start?"

"Start what, honey?"

"The murder investigation."

"Right." She tightened her lips and tapped her chin with her finger. "I think that we should start with the crime scene."

"That would be here," I said, and pointed my head toward the house.

"She may have died here, but that isn't where she was murdered."

"And how shall we deduce where exactly the crime took place."

"Only one way to find that out," she said. "And that's by going to talk to Viola Rose at the Jellybean Cafe."

Chapter Eleven

Saturday Morning, AGD (After Gemma Died)

Head lifted up, nose jutted forward, the aroma of freshly brewed coffee, sugary-sweet cinnamon rolls, and sizzling bacon lifted me out of my bed. I practically floated down the stairs and followed the mouthwatering whiff of her cooking through the house and into Renmar's Palace of Heavenly Delights (everyone else called it a kitchen).

I know I'd sworn off Renmar's cooking after Gemma died in a bowl of her bouillabaisse. And I know that it had only been one day (I wasn't even sure if the yellow caution tape had been removed from the stove), but I just couldn't resist. I had become addicted to her food and, just like a junkie, I was willing to risk my life for a fix.

Hi. My name is Logan, and I'm a Renmar Food Junkie . . .

I wonder if she has any of those fruit cups? I whispered as my flight ended and my feet gently landed in the middle of the kitchen.

"Good morning, Sunshine." Renmar smiled as I came in, she was stirring something in a metal bowl. "You hungry?"

"Yes, I am." I sat on one of the kitchen stools. "Good morning, Brie. Oliver." They were congregated around the island.

Brie reached over and rubbed my arm. "Good morning, Honeybun. How are you this morning?"

"Good," I said. "Hungry." I looked at Renmar.

"I'll get you something," she said. "But I think Mother wants you to have breakfast with her."

"So, Logan," Oliver said to me. He was puffing on one of his e-cigarettes. "I hear you and Miss Vivee are taking a drive?"

Odd looking didn't exactly describe Oliver Gibbons. He wasn't bad looking, and evidently had a way about him that made women go wild. To me, he looked like a man out of his time, of course making that e-cigarette he always had anachronistic. In the time I imagined he'd fit in, Oliver would have been considered "dapper." The kind to wear a seersucker suit and a straw hat, or pastel-colored plaid pants.

"Yes," I said to Oliver. "We're going for a drive." I didn't want to say too much about us going out because I didn't know what Miss Vivee had told them. I had come to Yasamee to make amends for being a liar, and the first thing I did was hook up with one.

"I heard she hasn't been out of the house for twenty years," I said. I picked up a banana from the bowl of fruit sitting on top of the island. "Is it okay if I eat this?" I asked Renmar.

"Help yourself," she said. "And I want you to know how much we appreciate you taking Mother out. I don't know what you did to her, but she is just so excited. Isn't she, Brie?"

Brie nodded.

"So you don't mind her going out?" I asked.

"Oh. No," Renmar said. "I'm happy that Mother is going to do something other than sit around here all day in her coat and hat, holding her pocketbook like she's waiting for McIntosh Funeral Home to come and pick her up." She smiled at me. "And I'm glad you're helping her out. She thinks she fooled me. Telling me she was going to help you out on the Island. It took no more than an accusatory '*Mother*' – drawing it out for emphasis, for her to spill the beans."

"She told you what we're really doing?"

"Of course she did." Renmar poured her mixture into cake pans. "She told me that she wanted to stop by the church and light a candle for Gemma Burke.

71

Pray for her soul. And maybe stop at the cemetery and put some flowers on Daddy and Louis' graves. Don't that just beat all?" She walked over to the oven and put her cake tins in.

That was just about as far from the truth as one could get.

"When she asked you to take her to the cemetery, she tell you about Louis?" Renmar asked.

"Uhm, not exactly," I said. It was the first I'd heard of him. In fact, it was the first I'd heard anything about going to a cemetery.

"Louis is my late husband, God rest his soul," Renmar continued. "Bay's father. The love of my life." She smiled at me. Her eyes appeared to have misted up. "I was thinking, Logan." She batted her eyes to make the tears go away. "If you wouldn't mind," she looked over at me, "can you take Mother over to the Jellybean Café? She loves their egg salad. It'll be such a treat. Not sure she'll want to stop, but you could try, couldn't you?"

Won't be too difficult to do since that's where we were going anyway.

"I'll try," I said instead.

"I'm surprised Momma didn't ask Bay to take her out," Brie said. "We only get to see him every blue moon. Seems like she'd want to spend the day with him."

"He couldn't," Renmar said. "He's riding with the Sheriff to accompany Gemma's body up to Augusta."

"How long is your son staying?" I asked Renmar as innocently as I could.

"A week maybe. Maybe a little longer."

Crap.

"He's on vacation," she continued. "And instead of going on a trip to a tropical island with a pretty girl on his side, he chose to come to Yasamee and see us. Ain't that nice?"

Just my luck.

"Miss Vivee is a very compassionate person," Oliver said, running his hand over his salt and pepper hair. "I'm not surprised she wants to light a candle for Gemma." He took a puff on his e-cigarette. He seemed to always have one in his hand. "Nice of you, Logan, to take her," he continued. "No one's died around here in ages. And seeing it right before your eyes can make a person want to make amends with their God."

"Oliver. Are you saying that my momma needs to reconcile something with God?" Brie seemed insulted.

He held up his hands. "No. Brie. We all know that Miss Vivee is a saint." He winked his eye at me.

Ha! I knew she wasn't, and I had just gotten to Yasamee.

"It's just at her age," he continued, "people like to have a good relationship with their maker, if they believe in such things."

"How old is Miss Vivee?" I asked.

"I'm not sure," Renmar said. "I think maybe eighty-nine, ninety. Somewhere about there." Renmar looked over at Brie. "Do you know exactly?"

"Not exactly. No," Brie said. "She claims to be a hundred. But I don't believe it."

"How could you not know?" I asked.

"It ain't polite around these parts to ask a woman her age," Brie said. "And, most women lie about it anyway."

"It makes us more appealing when we're mysterious. Didn't you know that, Logan?" Renmar asked.

I laughed. "No. I didn't know that."

"Well it does. And believe me its appealing to be one hundred. Everyone pays attention to you."

"However old she is," I said, "It sure hasn't slowed her down."

"Age ain't nothing but a number," Brie said and made Renmar and Oliver laugh.

"I don't know about that," I said.

"Honey, you must know that. How old are you?" Renmar asked.

"Twenty-eight."

"Close to thirty then, right?" Renmar said.

"Yep," I said.

"And I bet you don't feel like you're any older on the inside than you when you were sixteen or twenty, do you?"

"I used to think that thirty was old, but now that I'm almost there, to be honest I don't feel old," I admitted.

"And neither do I. Or Brie. Or Mother. We feel just like we did when we were young. On the *inside*. In our minds. It's just that our bodies aren't cooperating. I got a whole lot wiser in all these years, but all the things I've wanted and the way I felt when I was young haven't changed. Just because the years have passed. Things that young people want – happiness, nice things, love and wanting to be loved – are just a part of human nature. Doesn't matter how old you are."

"Renmar, my dear," Oliver said waving his fake cigarette around. "You missed your calling. You should have been a writer of prose."

"Go on now, Oliver. You're making me blush."

"Oliver," I said, "you're quite modern, smoking that e-cigarette."

"He thinks it'll save him from lung cancer," Brie said. "Started smoking them when Louis died."

Oliver studied his electronic cigarette and took a puff. "I can enjoy the menthol, get my nicotine fix, and not have any of the ill effects of tobacco," he said. "It's a modern miracle."

"Nonsense," Brie said.

Renmar went over to the sink. She washed her hands and gazed out of the window. "Looks like it's going to be a nice day to be outside."

"I had planned on going over to the Island today," I said. "That was before Miss Vivee asked me to take her to . . . uhm, church."

Oliver and Renmar looked at each other.

"What are you planning to do over there," Oliver asked. "It's been closed to the public a long time."

"I'm not the public," I said, trying not to sound impertinent. "Right now I just have permission to go and do noninvasive studies. But my mother has some contacts at the Archaeological Conservancy and she's working on getting me a permit to dig."

Renmar dropped a bowl on the floor. It clanged and bounced, and clanged some more. Everyone looked at her.

"Are you alright?" Brie asked.

"Just clumsy is all." Renmar glanced at Oliver. "Well. That's nice, Logan" she said. She stooped and picked up the bowl and threw it in the sink. "Isn't that nice, Oliver? That she gets to go over to the Island?"

He didn't say anything. He put his e-cigarette in a silver case, put it in his jacket pocket and picked up a bunch of grapes out of the fruit bowl. He plucked one and popped it in his mouth.

"Oliver's family owned most of the land in Yasamee." Renmar kept talking. "Including the Island. He's very rich. You'd never know it though, he's so humble. Doesn't flaunt his money." She smiled. "But I digress. Yes. He's very familiar with it." She looked at Oliver. "Aren't you, dear?"

"I'm not all that rich. Put me up next to Bill Gates or Warren Buffett, and I fade away like the shoreline at high tide. But, she's right," he said. "I am very knowledgeable about the Island. I could tell you whatever you wanted to know."

"Good," I said. "Maybe when I get over to the Island, you'll give me a guided tour."

"I'll be happy to," he said and shot a glance at Renmar. "You just let me know." He stood up and patted me on my back. "I've got to go. Brie, I've got a pretty lady meeting me here today. I need the best seat in the house."

"All the seats are the same," she said. "But I'll see what I can do."

"Have a good day, ladies." Oliver tipped an invisible hat and left, following Brie into the dining room.

"Is it a different woman he's having breakfast with?" I asked. "Different than the last three I've seen him with?"

Renmar laughed. "I know. And he claims he's in love with all of them."

Chapter Twelve

There was much fanfare with Miss Vivee leaving the house for the first time in twenty years. People were congratulating her on leaving and working on the Island. It was like Miss Vivee had been crowned Miss Yasamee and there was to be a parade in her honor. But no one knew the truth about why she was leaving the house.

Miss Vivee came down while I was still hanging out in the kitchen with Renmar. She made me eat breakfast in the kitchen with her. Then she took the rest of the morning to get ready, and said it was "real important" that she looked her best. Good thing too, because when we got out to the main part of the house, the dining room was full of people waiting to see her off.

She had on light pink lipstick, and a pink coat and hat that fit down over her head. She wore a checkered lavender and white dress and opaque beige stockings.

I just don't know how she doesn't have heat stroke. She wore a coat, granted a thin one, practically every day.

Her long hair had been pulled back into a braid and pinned up at the nape of her neck. Her "pocketbook," as she called it, on one arm, and Cat in tow, she made her entrance into the dining room like she was the Queen of England.

"Looks like everybody got wind of this momentous occasion," she muttered as we walked out. "I know Renmar and Brie are happy with all the customers."

"Is this all because we're going out?"

"This is all because *I'm* going out. Nobody gives two hoots and a holler what you do," she said. "But I could do without all of this." She waved her hand around and put a scowl on her face. "Wonder will this many people show up at my funeral."

Miss Vivee's scowl couldn't hide how pleased she was with the people who came to see her off. Even I could tell that.

"So how far does this Viola Rose live?" I asked after I got her and her dog in the car, calmed down, and buckled in. She didn't like my Jeep at all. Said it was too high off the ground. She fussed a good while about it.

"If I knew I was going to have to climb into the cab of an eighteen-wheeler, I would have called a taxi," she had said grumbling.

"Two blocks over." She pointed her finger. "Go that way. We're not going to her house. We're going to the diner, remember?"

"But -" I tried to protest. The way she pointed wasn't the way to the town square.

"You think you know this town better than me?" She glanced at me. "Because you don't."

"I'll go whichever way you want me to, Miss Vivee," I said, and followed her direction.

"In this quadrant," she said after sending me on a circuitous route and ending up on the other side of the square without going through it, "are streets named after trees. Ash, Oak, and that one coming up is Magnolia." She watched with anticipation as we came up on Magnolia. Halfway across it, she yelled, "Stop!" She said it so suddenly that it threw both of us forward when I hit the brakes.

"What's wrong?"

"I want to go down Magnolia," she said.

"That's why you yelled at me?" I mashed on the gas and turned the steering wheel hard to maneuver around the corner and go down the street I'd almost passed. "You could have caused us to have an accident."

"Accident?" She looked around out of all the windows. "There is not one car coming this way. Who were you going to run into?"

She got quiet and peered out of the window as I drove down the street, and in a barely audible voice she muttered, "I wonder does it still look the same."

"What did you say?"

"Nothing. Just keep driving."

I drove down the street. About midway down it, Miss Vivee cried out again, "Oh no!" She tried to crunch down in her seat. She was barely tall enough to see out of the window as it was. But she moved fast, bending her neck and trying to lean forward so she couldn't be seen through the passenger side window. I didn't think she was limber enough to get completely out of sight. And I do believe she would have dropped to the floor of the car if she could've.

"What?" I yelled again as I slammed on the brakes. "What's wrong now?"

"Oh. Good Lord, don't stop!"

I put my foot back on the gas.

"Hurry up! Get me out of here."

"What is wrong with you?" I glanced over at her as I maneuvered down the street.

"Nothing's wrong with me." She fixed her hat on her head and stretched her neck to peer out of the window. Looking back down the street, she asked, "Do you think he saw me?"

"Who?" I asked and looked in the rearview mirror. "That man with the cane walking his dog?"

"Yes! The man with the cane walking the dog. Did he see me?"

"I don't know, but he's still standing there, watching us drive away."

"Oh Lord Almighty. I think I'm gonna faint," she said and started fanning herself with her hand. Turn on the air, child."

"Who is he?" I asked as I put the fan on high and rolled up the windows. "Is he someone you know?"

"Can you just drive and not ask so many questions. All I did was ask you to go down Magnolia and before I know it you're making a big production number out of it."

"Me?"

"Drive to the diner," she huffed. "You think you can do that?" She strained to look out the back window as if to make sure we weren't being followed.

I checked the car mirror. "He's gone," I said.

"Who cares," she said and waved her hand at me. "Let's just get to what we come to do. The diner." She wagged her finger pointing out the windshield at the road ahead and nodded.

In other words, telling me to get a move on.

Chapter Thirteen

"Land sakes alive, it's true." A waitress met us at the door. "I do declare. Rumor mill said you were coming out, and dang blasted it if you ain't standing right here in my diner."

"Mornin' Viola Rose," Miss Vivee said, and waved her hand dismissing her comments. "You want to seat us, or just stand here and gawk? I can't leave my dog in the car all day while you gab."

Stepping into the Jellybean Café was like arriving in the Land of Oz. It was all in Technicolor. There were shiny chrome, bright red leather-topped stools, placed a few feet apart underneath an aluminum counter that ran the length of the restaurant. The booths were a vibrant red, turquoise, purple, and yellow stripes, with radiant white Formica table tops that matched the polished linoleum floor and were set in front of huge picture windows that sparkled with colorful neon signs.

"Gus, look who's here," Viola Rose called out. She grabbed two menus and headed toward one of the booths.

"Well, if it ain't the matriarch of Yasamee, Georgia." Gus grinned. "Rose, you make sure you treat her like royalty. Anything she wants, it's on the house."

"Don't you think I know what to do?" Viola Rose countered.

Gus, who could pass for a munchkin, was short, muscular and seemed to have a permanent scowl on his face. He worked the flattop grill with skill, donned in a white apron, t-shirt, and chef's skull cap. And if he was one of the citizens of Oz, Viola Rose was its good witch, Glenda. She was pink and bedazzled – shiny lips, shiny eyeshadow, and shiny rings on every finger. Even her eyes sparkled when she smiled. Her strawberry blond hair was teased high into a bouffant and she had several pens sticking out of it.

"How long has it been, Miss Vivee?" Viola Rose asked.

"Twenty years."

"Oh my! Don't that just beat anything?" Viola Rose stopped in her tracks. "You venture out after twenty years and you come to my diner." She loosed a smile that was as wide as the Mississippi. "Here, Miss Vivee." She walked over to a booth that sat in the center of one of the windows, a purple and pink sign blinking "Open" hanging in the middle of it. "You sit right here. This was always your favorite booth," Viola Rose said, patting the table.

"Now who you got with you? This Bay's girlfriend?" Viola Rose asked, eyeing me.

"Just because she black don't mean she's dating Bay, Viola Rose. I know lots of black people. She's an archaeologist," Miss Vivee said, seemingly proud. "And she consented to having lunch with me."

"Don't put words in my mouth, Miss Vivee," Viola Rose said. "I was only asking. Not making any judgments."

"Well, you ask too many questions," Miss Vivee said.

"You not gonna rile me today, Miss Vivee. I'm too happy to see you." Viola Rose pulled a pen out of her hair and an order pad out of her apron pocket. "So what can I get you ladies?"

"I'll have coffee, and she'll have an iced tea."

"I'll have a Pepsi, please," I said. "Lots of ice."

"It's a fountain drink, is that okay with you?" she asked.

"Yep," I said and picked up the menu. "You want egg salad, Miss Vivee?"

"Oh my God, no! Why would you think that?"

"I thought you liked my egg salad, Miss Vivee." Viola Rose frowned up her face.

"Just bring us our drinks, Viola Rose. Give me a chance to see what else you got."

"If you want answers from her," I leaned in and lowered my voice after Viola Rose left, "seems like you'd be a lot nicer to her."

"I'm going to need you to run over to Hadley's Drug store," she said ignoring me. "It's right there on the corner. See." She pointed out the window. "I want one of those small notebooks that the detectives use. You know it has the spiral wire on the top."

"I haven't ordered yet."

"Well order. Then go get me a notebook, please. And three No. 2 pencils. Already sharpened."

"Okay," I said. I sat and perused the menu for a while. Everything looked good. I remember Renmar telling me they had good food here. "What are you having?" I asked Miss Vivee.

"An egg salad sandwich," she said, impatiently tapping her fingers on the tabletop. She hadn't even looked at her menu. "Now. You tell me what you want and I'll tell Viola Rose while you go to Hadley's."

"Didn't you just say you didn't want any egg salad?"

"Are you going to tell me what you want so I can get it ordered for you?"

Geesh.

I let out a groan. "Okay. I'll do a cheeseburger and French fries."

"Okay then. Now go. Shoo. And hurry back."

Luckily Hadley's Drugstore had the notebook Miss Vivee wanted, but they didn't sell pencils that were already sharpened. I considered getting her a mechanical pencil, but when told the sales clerk who it was for, she wouldn't let me get one. She said she'd sharpen the pencils for me.

Miss Vivee controlled people with just the mention of her name.

"We should make a list of suspects," Miss Vivee said when I got back.

"That's a good idea," I said, then took a sip of my cola. Viola Rose had waited to bring it to me until I got back. Miss Vivee had downed half of her cup of coffee. "Did you order my food, Miss Vivee," I asked.

"Of course I did. You think I was just over here twiddling my thumbs?"

Miss Vivee pulled the notebook and pencils out of the plastic Hadley's Drugstore bag. She opened up the notebook and licked the tip of her pencil.

"Okay. Who we got so far?" she asked. Her shaky hand perched over the paper.

"You want me to write?" I asked.

"Why would I need you to write? I'm heading up this investigation. These should be my notes."

Before I could say anything, Viola Rose brought our food over.

"I put extra egg salad on there, Miss Vivee. "I knew you were only kidding when you said you didn't want any."

"I don't kid, Viola Rose. But I realized my outburst wasn't nice so I decided to eat some," she looked up at the waitress, "for the sake of your feelings."

Viola Rose shook her head.

"Okay, you two enjoy."

I put some ketchup on my fries, then some on my burger with a little mustard. I bit into it and the juice from the meat ran down my arm. "Oh man. This is good," I said through a mouth full of food. "You like your egg salad, Miss Vivee?"

"It's okay," she said.

"You want more coffee, honey?" Viola Rose came to the table with a steaming pot in her hand.

"No," Miss Vivee said and placed her palm on the top of the cup. "But I do want to ask you something."

"Anything you need."

"It's about Gemma Burke."

"Poor thing. I heard about what happened. Terrible thing that it happened at your place. I reckon that Renmar was just beside herself. 'Specially with the Sheriff having to confiscate her famous bouillabaisse."

"Sheriff ruffled her feathers with that one," Miss Vivee said. "She wants to make sure no one finds out her secret ingredients. And the thought of the county lab examining it practically sent her off her rockers."

Viola Ray set the coffee pot on the table, put her hands on her hips, and let out a laugh. "Renmar'd kill somebody over her recipes. Come to think of it, sort of a coincidence, Gemma asked me did I know how to make Renmar's bouillabaisse. She said she'd do anything to find out what's in it."

"Did she now?" Miss Vivee asked, seemingly intrigued.

"Tell me, Viola Rose, what do you know about her?"

"Who? Gemma Burke?" Viola Rose asked. "Probably no more than you. You remember her before she left here to go to the big city."

"Yeah, I do. But that was so long ago."

"Well, she hadn't changed much. She still was a nice girl. Quiet, but polite. She was always smiling." Viola Rose tilted her head upward and squinted her eyes like she was thinking. "I asked her once why she come back after she was so gung-ho to leave, and she told me she just missed home."

"So she hadn't changed much, huh?"

"No way I could tell. Only thing I know she did different was she had become what you call one of them, uhm . . . Runners."

"Joggers," Miss Vivee said and eyed me.

"Yeah. You know. But now that I think about it, she seemed quieter than before. Always keeping to herself. I thought about that when I used to see her running out there." She pointed through the window. "Always by herself."

"She'd run past here?" I asked.

"Yep. That was the last time I saw her. Going past my window. Every morning she'd come from her house and jog past here. She did it on the day she died."

"What time was that, Viola Rose?" Miss Vivee asked.

"I know exactly what time it was. Eleven thirty. Junior Appletree had come in for his lunch. Comes in everyday at the same time. Funny, how I noticed her that day. Can't say that I remember what time she ran by here any other day."

"But you do remember that she passed here every day," I asked.

"Sure do. Every day during the week. I don't think she ran on the weekend. Leastways, I can't say I remember her doing it."

"How'd she look when she passed?"

"How'd she look?" Viola Rose seemed puzzled.

"I mean was she coughing? Did she look like she was in any pain?"

"I can't say." She cocked her head to the side. "But I guess if she was coughing or sickly I would have taken notice of it." She looked down at Miss Vivee. "So. Nope. I'd have to say she wasn't. She looked like she did any other day."

"Wasn't she staying in Gunner Hadley's old house?" Miss Vivee asked.

"Yeah, she was renting it. You know she sold her parents' house when she left."

"Where did she go when she left here?"

"I don't rightly know." Viola tapped her chin with her finger. "She said 'big city.' I'm sure it was Augusta. You know I don't like to pry into people business."

"Yes, Viola Rose, I know," Miss Vivee said, obviously being sarcastic.

"She's got a girl staying up there at the house with her, though," Viola Rose added. "Brought her back with her when she came home."

"Really? I don't remember seeing any new faces around here?" Miss Vivee said.

"Sweetie, you ain't left the house in twenty years, probably a lot of things around here you ain't seen." She stuck her hands down in the pockets of her apron. "She's come in here to eat plenty of times. She's a real bump on a log. Mousey. Quiet. I always wondered what her and Gemma did together, because they wouldn't say two words to each other when they'd come in here to eat. But Gemma was real nice to her. Gemma would always pay for the food for the both of them."

"What's the girl's name?" Miss Vivee asked.

"Hmmm. Can't say I know." Viola Rose used one of the pens stuck in her hair to scratch her head. "Don't know if Gemma ever said it."

"Why was she staying with Gemma?" Miss Vivee asked.

"Well ain't you full of questions?"

"It happens when you don't get out much," Miss Vivee said matter-of-factly. "You just become overflowing with questions, almost to the point where you feel like you're gonna pop if you don't get them answered. Plus," Miss Vivee said and leaned forward to whisper to Viola Rose, "I want to help Renmar and the Maypop keep their good reputation." She touched her on the arm. "Like you said, it ain't good for her or our establishment if people are dying."

"Don't I know it. I just shudder at the thought of that happening here. Someone dying right in one of my booths." Her shoulders shuddered.

"That's why I came down here to talk to you, Viola Rose. I knew you could help me clear Renmar's good name."

"Miss Vivee. You know I'd do anything for you or your family." She bit down on her bottom lip. "No. I can't say that I ever heard either one of them say her name. But if something comes to mind, I'll let you know." Viola Rose crossed her arms in front of her. "And I don't know why that girl is living with her either." Viola Rose lowered her voice. "Can't say that either one of them ever told me the reason. But I was figuring she was broke. She seemed as useless as a screen door on a submarine."

"Has she been in here today?" Miss Vivee asked.

"No. She ain't been in here today." The door to the diner opened with a jingle. "I'll be right with you," Viola Rose called out to the couple that came in. "But I know she'll be here later," she said, then reached down and picked up Miss Vivee's coffee cup. "It's Saturday. I serve Shepard's Pie every Saturday and she never misses it."

The bell on the door jingled again. "Good Lord. Look like lunchtime rush done started." She patted Miss Vivee's hand. "I'll be back."

Chapter Fourteen

Miss Vivee pushed her plate back, which was completely devoid of even one morsel of egg salad and leaned her elbows on the table. "Well do you think any of that was useful information?" she asked me.

"Any of what?"

"Any of what Viola Rose said. Sometimes it's the most innocuous things that reveal the murderer."

I let my eyes drift upward.

Nothing had been revealed to me.

"I think what happened to her, happened along the route she took to jog," Miss Vivee said.

"What did happen to her?" I asked.

"In due time. I'll tell you in due time."

Fine. Moving on.

"I thought we were going to make a suspect list," I said instead.

"Oh, right," she said. She pulled out her pencil and pad. "Who we got?" She licked the granite tip.

"Uhm . . ." I gazed out of the window. "The Sheriff thinks it may have been Renmar." I shook my head. "But that was just him." I didn't want to insult her by her thinking I agreed with the sheriff that her daughter poisoned Gemma.

She licked the tip of the pencil again, I guessed for good measure. "Renmar Colquett."

"Are you putting her on our suspects list?"

"Sure am."

"Why?" I had to chuckle. "She's your daughter."

"Doesn't mean she's not a murderer. Renmar's got a mean streak in her. And she'd kill to keep her recipes secret. You heard Viola Rose, Gemma Burke wanted Renmar's bouillabaisse recipe." Miss Vivee licked her lips. "Renmar rather give up her left arm than divulge her recipes. And her bouillabaisse is famous. It's won awards."

"Yeah, I know about her being protective." I laughed. "She said that if she told me what she put in her fruit bowl, she'd have to kill me."

"See what I mean."

"I can't believe you'd put her down."

"You think she's protective about that fruit concoction, it's nothing compared to her bouillabaisse."

"But you said that the murder didn't happen at the Maypop."

"It didn't."

"Wasn't Renmar there all day?"

"Nope." She said. She picked up her cup of coffee and took a sip. "She went out early. Stayed a couple of hours. Came back with Oliver. The two of them had their heads together about something."

"The murder?"

"It's possible."

"They were acting strange when the Sheriff was there."

"Yep. And Renmar had Oliver dump that pot of bouillabaisse. That's why she told Sheriff Haynes there wasn't any."

"But if the bouillabaisse didn't kill Gemma, why would Renmar and Oliver get rid of it?"

"I don't know. That's why her name is going on the list."

"Then what about Oliver?" I asked. "He and Renmar may be accomplices. He is pretty shady guy with all of his 'lady friends'."

Miss Vivee shook her head. "Not Oliver. He's practically family."

"Renmar *is* family and her name is on your list." I pointed to her "detective notebook," every page blank save for the lone sheet that had the name of her daughter on it.

"I know Oliver," she said taking another sip of the cold coffee and swallowing. "He is a gentle soul. Wouldn't hurt a fly. He and Brie had a thing once upon a time. And the only mischief I've ever known him to get into is what Renmar puts him up to. Then you know he and Hazel Cobb are related and Renmar and Hazel are related. So that makes him family. He's not the murderer."

"Renmar and Oliver? They're related to Hazel Cobb?"

"Yes."

I didn't say anything and I guess she must've seen by the look on my face that I was having problems with putting that genealogy together.

"Oliver's great-great-great – I hope I put enough greats in there – grandfather is Hazel Cobb's great-great-great grandfather on the slavery side. And Bay's father, Renmar's husband, Louis, was Hazel's cousin."

"Bay's father is Hazel's cousin on . . . On the slavery side?"

"No," she said and slowly wiped her mouth with the napkin and then pressed it out on her lap. She met me eye to eye. "You know, sometimes your lack of understanding is just scary," Vivee said. "You're going to have to try to keep up, otherwise you won't be much help to me." She took another sip of the cold coffee. "Bay's father was black. You couldn't tell that?"

"Yes. I – I was just trying to understand," I stumbled over my words. It was hard staying nice and respectful when the other person was acting out.

"Understand what? Slavery?" she asked.

"No. I get that."

"Then what are you confused about, honey?" She pushed back her cup of coffee and folded her hands on the table. She leaned in and spoke slowly. "Renmar married a black man. The black man was Hazel's cousin. Hazel is also black. And way, waaayy back, her family was owned by Oliver's family. Is that clear enough for you, Missy?"

"Never mind. I get it."

I changed the subject.

"So if the murderer was out somewhere." I waved my hand. "That means the entire town could be on the list."

"That's not how it works. Don't you watch crime shows? Do the people on Law & Order ever put every single citizen of New York on the suspect list?" She clucked her teeth. "No. We have to narrow it down."

"How do we do that?"

"I think I know what to do."

The bell jingled on the door and it made me look up.

"Oh look who just came in?" I said.

"Who?" Miss Vivee tried to turn around and look.

"The man with the cane and the dog."

"Lord have mercy," she said and again tried to make herself invisible by sliding down in her seat. "What is he doing here?"

"Getting something to eat I would guess," I said and leaned over to her. "Now who's showing a lack of understanding?"

"Shush!" she said.

"Here he comes," I said.

"What! No!"

I watched as he walked past our table. He'd left his cane at home and was doing all he could to walk tall without it. He had a slight limp. I was thinking he probably should have brought his cane along. He looked as old as Miss Vivee and hidden under the lap of skin over his eyes, he had the brightest blue eyes that seemed to sparkle when they landed on her. As he passed us, he slowed and nodded his greeting to me and spoke to Miss Vivee.

"Vivienne," he said.

"Mac," she countered back not even looking up.

He walked to the end of the counter and took a seat on the very last stool.

Miss Vivee could hardly catch her breath. She put her hand over her forehead. "Driving down Magnolia might not've been such a good idea," she muttered. "Could we please leave now?" She put the notebook and pencils in her purse.

"Who is he? Your boyfriend?" I leaned in and asked with a big grin on my face.

"Don't be silly. I'm too old to have a boyfriend."

"Well, he must be somebody." I said looking over my shoulder at him and then back at Miss Vivee. "Got you upset."

"I'm not upset. And," she said scooting to the edge of her seat ready to go. "We have too much to do to dilly-dally around here all day."

"I'm not leaving until you tell me who he is. What's his name? Is it Mac?"

She huffed and fiddled with her purse. "Macomber Whitson," she said giving in. "But everyone calls him Mac. Now can we go?"

Chapter Fifteen

Saturday Afternoon, AGD

Miss Vivee sat down in the car seat with a huff. Seeing Mac had seemed to really upset her. Even Cat crawling up front and plopping down on Miss Vivee's lap didn't get a rise from her. Her face was twisted, her wrinkles sagged more than I'd ever seen them, and she seemed to have drifted off, staring out of the windshield.

I thought maybe I shouldn't have given her such a hard time about that guy. He evidently meant something to her, or had meant something to her.

I noticed that Miss Vivee always called people by two names. If they didn't have two first names, Miss Vivee would call them by their first and last name. She did that to everyone but family – Renmar, Brie and Bay (she didn't usually call me by name, she'd just sort of talked at me, and when she did use a name it was Missy). And now this man was just "Mac."

Mac must be like family to her.

I looked over at her sitting there, and it seemed almost like she was sad. Cat had placed her paws on Miss Vivee's chest and put her wet nose right in her face, trying to get her attention. But Miss Vivee didn't seem to pay her any notice. I remembered what Renmar said, it doesn't matter how old you are, you still have the same wants and desires. You always feel the same inside, she had said.

I guess that went for Miss Vivee and Mac.

Cat gave up, climbed into the backseat, and I reached over Miss Vivee and grabbed her seatbelt. I buckled her in and decided I was going to be more sensitive to her. Maybe getting back to the Maypop would make her feel better.

"You've got to get me a newspaper." She said suddenly.

"What?" I asked in surprise. "Why do you need me to get you a newspaper? There's one at the Maypop, isn't there?" I remembered seeing one that morning.

"Home?" she turned to me and tilted her head. "Why in the world would I be ready to go home?" She shook her head and closed her eyes as if tolerating me was such a chore. "Look," she said opening her eyes.

"We got some staking out to do, but first I want to go and find the crime scene." She reached in her purse and pulled out her sunglasses.

"I thought we did that when we went over to talk to Viola Rose at the diner."

"We just learned about the crime scene. We didn't actually go to it, now did we?" She turned around and smiled at her dog. "What'cha doing back there, girl? Come here and give me a kiss."

Cat jumped up front and I rolled my eyes.

I hopped out of the car and went back to Hadley's where I'd bought her notebook and got her a newspaper.

"Where to?" I asked when I got back in the car. I turned the ignition.

"Mims Point Park. Over by the beach."

I drove around the square and headed over to the coastline of the Savannah River.

"I'm sure that's where she would have gone down to the run along the shoreline," Miss Vivee said.

Once we reached the park, Miss Vivee directed me to pull over near a set of sandstone steps that lead from the park down to the beach. I shut off the engine and we sat for ten minutes or so and watched as people walked and played. At least that's what I did. Miss Vivee seemed lost in thought, either that or she was having one of her senior moments when she would seem to fix her gaze on something far off and not know what was going on around her.

"Yasamee isn't that big," she said.

Yep, must've been a senior moment. I didn't know what she was talking about.

I tilted my head and looked at her sideways. "You okay, Miss Vivee?"

"Why wouldn't I be okay?" She broke her trance-like stare and furrowed her brow. "You know. If you don't straighten up, I'm going to have to demote you from partner to just driver."

I laughed. Pointing out the window I said, "So this is the crime scene."

"Possibly," she said and surveyed the area. "Wherever it was, there has to be something hard. Those steps would be just about right."

I followed her gaze. Miss Vivee hadn't told me how Gemma died, and I hadn't bought into the idea that she'd been murdered yet, but Miss Vivee seemed to know exactly what she was looking for.

"Viola Rose said that Gemma Burke ran past the Jellybean around 11:30 am."

"Yep. She said she remembered exactly because one of her customers that came in at the same time she saw her and he always comes for lunch at 11:30."

Miss Vivee nodded. "Junior Appletree. He works over at the library, doing cleaning and odd jobs. He eats there every day, breakfast, lunch and dinner. Viola Rose always bragging about how he can't get enough of her good cooking and the only thing that keeps him away is the Lord." Miss Vivee smiled. "What she don't know is that he eats all of his desserts at the Maypop, and Renmar always saves him a plate of our food on Sundays."

"So what time did Gemma get to the Maypop?" I asked.

"About one o'clock."

"Sooo, it was an hour and a half from the time she was seen running past the diner until the time she went to get some of Renmar's bouillabaisse."

"Yes," Miss Vivee said. "And she wasn't coughing when she passed by the diner. So I wonder . . ." she looked at me curiously. "How long does it take to run from the Jellybean Café to here and back to the Maypop?" Then she didn't say anything else. She just smiled at me and stared.

I didn't say anything either.

"I wonder . . ." she said again.

"Oh no!" I realized what she wanted. "I'm not jogging around Yasamee so you can work out your timeline of death. No."

"Why not? All the young people do it I hear. It'll help you stay in shape."

"I have a better idea. What's her address?" I punched the button to bring my GPS on screen. "I can find out how many miles it is on here. Then I can divide the average number of minutes it takes to jog a mile, and that'll give me how many minutes it takes to get here from the diner." I waited for her answer.

"I don't know her address," she said. "What is that thing?" She wiggled her finger at the GPS.

"Never mind." I turned the ignition. "Do you know how to get there? We'll use the odometer. We can just do it the old fashioned way."

Chapter Sixteen

"There's Gemma Burke's house." Miss Vivee pointed. "The yellow and white one. There. Slow down, now," Miss Vivee instructed. "Don't get too close."

I turned off the ignition and checked the odometer. "Okay," I said. "So it was four miles from the entrance to the beach to Gemma's house. There and back would be eight miles." I looked at Miss Vivee. "I don't think she'd run eight miles."

"Why?"

"That's just a lot of running. And if she went down those steps, the ones you say lead to the river, then that would add even more distance if she jogged along the beach. And sand is taxing to jog on."

"Okay. Maybe you're right. Viola Rose didn't mention that she'd ever seen her come back. Maybe she didn't run back. She ran that far and walked home."

"No," I said. "I didn't mean that. I think that she may have not run as far as the beach."

"Mmm hmmm," she said lost in thought. She took her sunglasses off, dug in her purse and pulled out her prescription glasses and put them on. Then she put her sunglasses on top of them.

"Need both?"

"I can't see details as far as the house without my prescription glasses and the sun bothers my eyes. I need to get a look at those steps."

"They do make prescription sunglasses, you know."

"Sometimes you're not as smart as you try to let on," Miss Vivee said with a grimace. "Why would I pay good money for another pair when I already have a pair of both?"

I didn't understand most of Miss Vivee's logic. And I figured most people wouldn't either. It was so hard to get her to see any other way but her own, and I just wasn't raised to argue and disrespect old people.

"Here," Miss Vivee said and handed me part of the newspaper she had me buy. "We can use this for cover."

I took the newspaper from her. "Do what now?"

She opened up the newspaper and flapped it, holding it in front of her face. "You don't know much about surveillance do you? We're going to watch out for Gemma Burke's roommate."

Ooooh. We're supposed to hide behind it.

"I do know that this girl – her roommate – doesn't know us from Adam," I said defiantly, not raising the paper. "Or that we're here watching for her."

"You don't know what she knows," Miss Vivee said. "And as soon as we find out her name she's going on the suspect list. That means she's dangerous. So unless you want to be the next one falling into a bowl of stew, you'd better be careful." She rattled the newspaper. "C'mon now. Get with it." She hit me on my elbow.

I reluctantly put the paper up. It was the obituary section.

"Now what?"

"We wait."

"Do we know what time she might leave to go to the Jellybean Cafe?" I asked. I really didn't want to sit for hours looking at the faces of dead people.

"Nope. But Viola Rose says she doesn't miss coming, and she hadn't been there yet. I'm guessing since we didn't see her on the way over, she's still in the house."

"We were at the park for a long time," I offered.

"We wait," she said.

"We don't even know what she looks like." My voice was leaning toward pouty.

"I do," Miss Vivee said.

"How? You've never seen her."

"That's right, Missy, but I've seen every other person in this town so she'll be the only one in Yasamee that'll be a stranger to me."

Even without Miss Vivee leaving the house in the past twenty years, I was positive that she would know Gemma Burke's roommate. Renmar had told me on my first day that everyone in Yasamee comes to the Maypop to eat.

So we sat, with the car running, windows rolled up, air conditioner on, and our faces hidden behind newspapers. Cat sat on her hind paws, most of the wait, staring out of the window, evidently not in need of a disguise.

"There she is!" Miss Vivee whispered, a big grin crawling across her face. She started rattling her paper. "It's her. You see? It's her!"

"Why are you whispering?" I asked. "She can't hear you."

"Hush!" was her reply.

We watched as Gemma's houseguest came out of the house, pulled the door closed behind her and headed toward the town square. Presumably to the Jellybean Cafe.

"Now what are we going to do?" I asked.

"I'm going to get into that house and see what I can find." She stuffed both pairs of glasses in her purse and nodded at me.

"It's locked. How are you getting in?"

"Did you see her lock that door? No! You didn't. She just pulled it shut. Pay attention. Us being investigators means we have to be observant."

"Wait," I said and grabbed her arm. "Maybe I should go."

"What? Why?" She frowned making the wrinkles on her face come closer together. "You wouldn't know what to look for."

"You can tell me what to look for," I replied. "Although, I don't think it would be that hard to figure out."

"I'm going," she said with a determined grunt and grabbed the door handle. "We don't have time to dilly-dally. She'll be back soon enough. I'll be out faster than two shakes of a lamb's tail."

She grabbed the door handle, trying to push open the door. It was too heavy for her. "I'll just slide in there quick like and have a look around." She finally got the door opened, but then turned and looked at me. "Well are you going to help me get out of this contraption?"

"I thought maybe you were just gonna 'slide' out of it."

Miss Vivee snorted and I knew that was my cue not to give her any more lip about it. I climbed out the car and went around to her side. I held out a hand. "C'mon. I've got you."

Miss Vivee got out and straightened her clothes. Cat hopped from the back across the front seat and out of the car door. "You wait here. If you see her coming back, you whistle," she said. "You know how to whistle, don't you?"

"Now you're quoting famous movies?"

"Can you whistle?" she asked again somewhat annoyed.

"Yes I can. I whistle and then what?"

"Then I come running out that house like a bat outta hell, hop in the car and you put the pedal to the metal, that's what."

"Gotcha," I said and closed her car door. I was trying to picture Miss Vivee, at ninety-something and five-foot-nothing, running out of the house quick enough for someone walking up not to see her. Then I tried to picture her running, period.

I just couldn't process that thought.

I went back around the car and sat behind the steering wheel and watched as Miss Vivee crossed the lawn and took the steps, one at a time, with her dog right beside her. When she got on the porch, it appeared that she had an epiphany and she turned around and headed back down the steps.

One at a time.

What is she doing?

Cat seemed just as confused as I was. "Are we going in or not?" the terrier seemed to say. She went up to the door, sniffed at it and turned to look at Miss Vivee, her tail wagging. Miss Vivee was still making her way down the steps.

I put my hand on the door handle. Maybe I should get out and see about the two of them. Perhaps she'd thought better of going in Gemma Burke's house and was coming back to the car.

But instead of coming back down the sidewalk, she went around back.

And stayed back there for a while.

Long enough that I started to get nervous.

I checked my rearview mirror. The girl could have eaten a seven course meal in the time that Miss Vivee had been gone.

I craned my neck to look down the long drive. No sign of her or that dog.

She said faster than two shakes of a lamb's tail?

She must've been talking about a dead lamb.

With each minute that slowly ticked by, the knot in my stomach cinched tighter and tighter. It was affecting my breathing and I could feel little beads of sweat forming on my forehead.

I gripped the steering wheel and laid my head on it. Maybe I should go and check on her.

How could I be so stupid to let her go in there?

If that FBI guy knew what I was doing with his grandmother . . .

Oh. My. God.

Bay Colquett would make sure that when I finished my federal time for trespassing at Track Rock Gap and lying to a federal officer, I'd do jail time in Yasamee County. I could hear the judge – "Guilty," he'd say as his gavel struck the top of his bench. "Breaking and entering, trespassing on private property, aiding and abetting . . . Guilty. Guilty. Guilty."

Crap.

Chapter Seventeen

I just couldn't wait any longer. I had counted the number of window panes on the front and side of Gemma's house, the number of yellow roses climbing up the trellis on her front porch, the number of houses from hers to the corner, both ways, and all the ones on the other side of the street. Twice. I calculated how long it would take an average jogger to run from Gemma's house to Mims Point Park, Maypop B & B, and the Jellybean Café. Then I had made a mental list of all of the four and five-letter words I could make by rearranging the letters in Gemma Burke's name. I was working on six-letter words – *gemmae*, that was an easy one – *embark, meager, eureka, bummer, rebuke, umbrae, umbrage, rummage* . . .

Wait. Those last two are seven letters.

I slammed my palms on the steering wheel.

This is ridiculous.

I pulled on the door handle and jumped out of the car. I broke into a trot when I rounded the front of the car and headed down the driveway. I didn't get ten feet down it when Miss Vivee and Cat appeared from around back of the house.

She was smiling and waving a paper in the air.

Oh Lord. Now they're going to add theft to the charges against me.

"What do you have?" my voice a low, raspy whisper.

"What? I can't hear you," she said. Then she held up her index finger telling me to wait a minute.

"Yoo-hoo," She yelled toward the house next to Gemma's.

"What are you doing?" I was about to freak out. Was she letting the neighbors know we'd just committed a whole slew of felonies?

Up went that finger again.

"Yoo-hoo. MayBelle. You home?" she said in a sweet, sing-songy voice.

By this time she was standing to the side of – MayBelle's – I guessed, porch, but still in Gemma's driveway. I jerked my head around to check and make sure The Roommate hadn't made her way back from the diner. And jerked it back to look at Miss Vivee. She seemed oblivious to the fact we might get caught and was concentrating on getting "MayBelle" out of the house.

I heard a screen door swing open. I just wanted to dive behind the azalea bushes and hide.

What was she doing?

"Well, I say. If it ain't Vivienne Pennywell," the rotund woman clad in a flowered peach duster exclaimed as she pushed herself out the door and came to the edge of the porch. "What are you up to?"

Now we had witnesses.

"And who is that you have with you?"

"That's Cat. My dog." Cat let out a yelp.

"No I mean the young woman." She looked down the driveway at me.

"That's Logan Dickerson. She's an archaeologist from Ohio," Miss Vivee said stuffing the paper she'd purloined from the house into her purse. "She's down here to do some work on Stallings Island."

They won't even have to put me in a line up. Miss Vivee just gave that woman all my vital statistics.

"Logan Dickerson, huh?" MayBelle, committing my name to memory, eyed me suspiciously. "That's a nice jeep she's got," she said pointing to my car. "My Jimbo's got one just like it. Only it's black." She looked at me. "White's a nice color, though."

May as well just take down the license plate number.

"And how is your boy, MayBelle? He got himself a wife yet?" Miss Vivee seemed to let her comment out with a snicker.

"Oh no." she said smiling. "He's still here with me."

"Figures," Miss Vivee mumbled. "MayBelle," Miss Vivee spoke louder. "I was trying to pay my respect to Gemma's houseguest." She wagged a thumb back toward Gemma's house. "But it seems like no one's home."

"She goes up to Jellybean's on Saturdays for Viola Rose's Shepard's Pie," MayBelle said.

"Dang it," Miss Vivee said and snapped her fingers. "I so wanted to tell her how bad I felt about Gemma's passing. I understand that's her cousin from up north."

How does she come up with this stuff?

"Wherever did you hear that from?" MayBelle said. She leaned on the porch's banister and did what she thought was whispering, but I could hear her clearly from where I stood.

"They ain't no relation, not by blood anyway." She leaned in further. "I think they may be partners." She almost mouthed the last word.

"Partners?"

"Yes. You know." She cocked her head and winked. "C'mon Miss Vivee, you aren't that behind the times, are you?"

"Oh," Miss Vivee said and nodded her head. "Well to each its own, I always say. What's her name, MayBelle? Gemma Burke's *partner*?"

"I can't say that I know."

"Well. I guess I'll see her at the funeral." Miss Vivee feigned disappointment.

"You going?" Maybelle asked.

"Of course I am. I delivered that girl. Brought her into this world. I couldn't miss her home going services." She started walking down the driveway, Cat at her heels and threw her hand up in a wave without looking back. "See you around, MayBelle."

I opened the passenger car and Cat scrambled into the car without any help. Miss Vivee required a push.

"We might have to get another car," she said after I got into the car. She gave me a sideways glance. "This one is too high for me."

"Did you really deliver Gemma Burke?" I asked, ignoring her comment.

"No! Goodness no." Miss Vivee frowned. "I couldn't stand her momma. I would have thrown up if I had had to see that women's innards during childbirth."

"So why did you say that?"

"In case MayBelle starts mouthing off to Gemma Burke's houseguest. She'll think I really had a reason to come over and won't think I was just snooping."

I let my eyes roll upward.

"So, this is an interesting twist, huh?" I said. "Gemma and the girl."

"Oh. Phooey," Miss Vivee said. "They weren't partners. That girl was straight as an arrow."

"You knew what she meant?" I said starting up the car and putting on my seatbelt.

"Of course I knew what she meant. You think they just made gay people yesterday?" She pulled her seatbelt across her and I took it and buckled her in. "Gemma Burke didn't swing that way," she said and pursed her lips. "Gemma dated plenty *men* before she left town. And Colin Prichard was sweet on her since the both of them were knee high to a grasshopper."

Ah, the cute deputy.

I guessed he probably wouldn't chase after a girl he didn't have a chance with. But I didn't know him that well. Yet.

"People can change," I said.

"She didn't." She dug down in her purse. "I found this." She whipped out a folded piece of paper with a flourish and a smile.

"What is that?"

"A love letter."

"Let me see." I took the letter from her and gave a sideway glance. Who would have guessed she was such a criminal.

What she'd found was a letter, addressed to "Gemma Bear" from a Jeffrey Beck. He was pouring his heart out in the letter saying he couldn't live without her and he'd do whatever it took to win her back, including he wrote, leaving his wife, Miranda.

"This isn't a love letter, Miss Vivee."

"It's about love and it's a letter. *Ipso facto*, it's a love letter. That gives us two more suspects," she said pulling out her notebook and a pencil giving the tip of it a lick.

"Who?"

"Jeffrey and Miranda Beck."

"A love triangle?" I nodded my head. "It makes sense." I don't think I've met them," I said.

Five hundred eighty three residents weren't a lot, but I didn't see how I'd ever meet all of them. Soon, I was sure, the thrill for Miss Vivee of being Miss Marple would fade, and I'd be on Stallings Island. Or going home.

Either one was fine with me.

"The Becks don't live in Yasamee."

"Oh," I said. "Where do they live?"

"Don't know. Found the letter tucked inside her drawer. Her *panty* drawer." She wiggled her eyebrows at me. "That means she still had feelings for him."

"It does?"

"Sure it does. Women only keep things men gave them in their underwear drawer if they like them." She looked at me. "There or a box that you keep all of your special mementos of him in." She nodded. "If you didn't like a man and he gave you something, what would you do with it?"

I hunched my shoulders. "I'd throw it away."

"Exactly," she said with a nod.

Her eyes fixed, she let her hand hover over her notebook. "But what I want to know is why the two of them were so secretive about this girl's name. She eats at Viola Rose's every week, and lives next door to MayBelle Hutchinson, the two biggest gossips in Yasamee. Heck in Augusta County. And neither one of them knows her name."

"We could just ask her her name," I suggested.

"Don't be silly. We'll ask Mae Lynn to find out for us."

"Who is Mae Lynn?"

"She's the dispatcher over at the Sheriff's office."

"How will she find out her name?"

"We're going to file a complaint. Say we saw some suspicious happenings at the house. The Sheriff will go and check it out. She'll have to tell him her name."

"Uhm . . ." I squinted my eyes. I wasn't exactly following her line of reasoning. "Wouldn't the Sheriff go and question her anyway? She was Gemma's roommate, it stands to reason that she might know something about her death."

"The Sheriff might not know she had a roommate. And he hasn't determined yet that Gemma Burke was murdered, and if he's beginning to lean toward that conclusion he thinking it was Renmar's bouillabaisse that killed her. He's got no reason to go looking for clues at her house. Not yet anyway."

"And we do?"

She let out a groan. "Of course we do," she said with some agitation. "Because her house could be where the crime occurred." She ran her hand over Cat's head and let her gaze drift out the front window of the car. "Even though I didn't see anything that could be the murder weapon. Still. This girl might have something to do with it."

"Is she going on the suspect list?"

"How can I put her on the list when I don't know her name?" She shook her head, threw Cat toward the back seat, pushed the notebook down into her purse, and sucked her teeth. "Home, please," she said and put on her sunglasses.

Chapter Eighteen

Sunday Morning, AGD

Miss Vivee's first day out in twenty years took a bigger toll on her than expected. She decided to sleep in late, a rare occurrence I was told, but it gave me the morning free. I decided it was time for me to visit Stallings Island.

I drove to Mims Point Park where Miss Vivee and I had been the day before. I parked the car and walked down the stone steps, wondering all the while was it really the way Gemma had come the day she died.

I ambled through the tall blades of sea oats that grew out from the patches of sand, and along the marshy shoreline of the Savannah River. The oats grew high over the morning glories, and saw palmetto scattered about. I breathed in the moist air and exhaled.

Perhaps I was meant to come here. To Stallings Island. I had had only one real job as an archaeologist and that was as the lead of an excavation team in Belize. I'd stumbled on a stone slab with a message written in Mayan hieroglyphs that lead me to previously undiscovered underground tunnels that ran from Panama to Guatemala. But I was never able to share my find with the scientific community because what I found was connected to the whole Mars Origin Theory my mother had discovered. Plus, I learned that I had only been put in charge of the excavation as part of a setup. A crazed man had wanted to kill my mother and used me to lure her in. He knew, with me being young and inexperienced, that being the lead member of an excavation team would be too much for me and I would call in my mother. Of course I did just that. And because I did, I saw a man get killed and my mother and I got kidnapped.

Life's too short. Gemma Burke's death is proof of that.

As I walked past two weathered boats moored in the sand, I wondered if I'd ever be an archaeologist that would make a significant contribution without being in the shadow of my mother. I wondered would I ever be as insightful and scientific as she was. The youngest, I was the only one of her three children that followed in her profession – my brother, Micah was a lawyer, and the oldest, my sister, Courtney was a teacher – and I know it made my mother proud that I was an archaeologist, and it made her want to help me that much more. But I just wanted to do something on my own. Not be the "baby" anymore.

Maybe this was it. Stallings Island.

My chance to shine.

There was so much history on the small island, but maybe, just maybe that small island had a big connection to a possible Maya migration. And if I found something here, on my own, not connected to my mother in any way . . .

Wouldn't it be something if I discovered there was?

That's probably the reason I risked trespassing on Track Rock Gap. I had something to prove.

Once I started college, I spent all my time preparing to become an archaeologist and to make a mark in the field. I didn't take time out to date, go out, or do any of the things most women my age did. I didn't have many friends that were married, but they all found the time to have men in their lives. Maybe I wouldn't be so "uptight" as my father says about being a famous archaeologist if I took some time out for myself. By that he meant to date.

And maybe my father was right. Gemma Burke gave up on love, albeit the guy was married, but she had taken a chance on it. But for some reason she came back home, moved some unknown girl in with her and then, according to Miss Vivee, got herself killed. Her life over, and my father would say, with nothing to show for it.

Maybe it's time I took my father's advice.

My father wrote a syndicated sports column. He and my mother had been married for more than thirty-five years. Most fathers are leery of their daughters dating, no man's good enough. Not my father. Andrew Mase Dickerson, called Mase by all, was gung-ho on his baby girl finding a man.

With my mother believing in Martians, my daddy trying to marry me off and all the other craziness I had to deal with growing up in my house, it's no wonder I took to Miss Vivee and her outrageous schemes.

As I rambled along the shore, the waves of the river's blue water brushed lazily upon the sand and I spotted the shoal that led over to the Island. It wasn't more than a couple yards from Oliver's beachfront house.

I knew I was still young and that if fame and fortune was what I wanted, I picked the wrong profession. So, I was okay with not having it. I just wanted to make a contribution. I just didn't want to end up like Gemma Burke – dead before my time.

I don't know why I hated to admit it, although I used this fact whenever I needed to, but my mother was very successful. There weren't many in our field that were as accomplished as she was. Yet, she was so down to earth. So normal. I knew that I'd never make a find as big as the one my mother had made, but if I could be just as good . . .

I stepped timidly across the shoal, the fishy odor abruptly invading my nostrils. I found myself holding my breath, arms out to keep my balance and anticipating what may lay on the Island for me to discover.

I was so excited.

Unfortunately the first thing I found when I got there was Renmar and Oliver. I ducked behind a tree and thought about what to do. They had been so secretive since Gemma's death. And even before that conspiratorial.

What if they really were the killers?

I turned around and went back to the Maypop.

Chapter Nineteen

Sunday Afternoon, AGD

"Mae Lynn called me this morning," Miss Vivee said in a strained whisper. She grabbed my arm and pulled me into the closet under the stairs as soon as I walked in the door from Stallings Island.

I didn't even know there was a closet there.

I twisted myself around in the small space. It was pitch black and even with Vivee's small frame it was tight for the both of us. "You couldn't tell me that out there?" I said bumping my head on the angled ceiling. I had taken to whispering too.

"No. I don't want nobody else to hear. Renmar is still a suspect you know."

"I just saw Renmar over on the Island," I protested. "She's not even here."

My eyes adjusted to the dark and I felt around on the wall by the door for a light switch, but found the light bulb was attached to a long cord that hung from the ceiling. I yanked on it and a beam of light broke up the darkness.

"What did Mae Lynn say?" I said in a regular voice.

Miss Vivee reached up and jerked the chain turning the light back off. "Shush. Not so loud." I could hear her breathing hard. "I wrote it down in my notebook." She started moving around. I could tell she was fiddling around with her purse.

"Oh shoot," she said. "I can't read it in here, it's too dark, dang it. That's okay, I remember what she told me."

"Well, what did she say?"

"She said that the girl is from Atlanta, her name is Koryn Razner. And it looks like Gemma Burke had lived there for a while too. So maybe that's where they met."

"How come we can't have any light?"

"I don't want anyone to know we're in here."

I couldn't argue with that.

"We have to talk to Colin Pritchard," she said.

"The deputy?"

"Do you know another Colin Pritchard?"

I guess I didn't.

"He went to Atlanta to do his Peace Officer training. Would've been there the same time that Gemma Burke was there."

"I thought you told me that he did his training up north?"

"Ain't Atlanta north of here?"

"Yeah, but I thought you meant the real north. Like Ohio." I shook my head. "Never mind."

"Can you take me over to see him?" she asked.

"On a Sunday?"

"You think the Sheriff's office takes a day off?"

"Sure," I agreed. "I'll take you."

Anything to get out of this closet.

"Are we telling Renmar the truth about where we're going?" I asked.

"Of course not." She groped around and found my arm and patted it. "But you leave the lying up to me."

"Okay."

"Okay," she repeated. "Now when we go out, just act natural."

Right.

I turned the knob and opened the door, my eyes adjusting back to the sudden flood of light saw a large figure standing in front of me. Turning my face to the side, squinting, I saw out of the corner of my eye that the big, looming figure was Bay. He had that stupid smirk smeared across his face.

Crap.

"What are you doing in the closet?" he asked.

"I was in there with Miss Vivee," I said in my defense.

Didn't he see her?

"Hello, Grandson."

"Hello, Grandmother. Aren't you looking lovely today?"

"Thank you," she said and wrapped her hand around his arm. "Logan was giving me a little training," she said.

"Training?" Bay looked at me questioningly.

"Yes, dear. You know for when I help her with her work. She said that I might have to go inside of caves and down through tunnels." She was making gestures with her free hand. "It'll be very dark in those places. So she said I needed to get used to being in small, dark spaces." She looked up at him and smiled. "Quite ingenious, don't you think? Making me stand in the closet."

How does she come up with these things?

"Ingenious isn't the word I'd use, Grandmother." He gave me a scowl.

"That is *not* why we were in that closet," I said.

"Then what were you doing in there with my grandmother?" he asked.

According to Miss Vivee I couldn't tell him the truth. So I said nothing. Clearly my imagination wasn't as advanced as Miss Vivee's.

"Are you okay?" Bay asked his grandmother.

"Oh yes, dear," she said as they walked away. "I just feel a little faint."

She turned back and winked at me.

He turned back and mouthed something that looked like, "You are sooo going to jail."

Oh crap.

Chapter Twenty

Colin Pritchard, good looking man that he was, looked even better in his civvies.

After we got rid of Bay, which took the better part of an hour, I drove Miss Vivee to the Sheriff's office to find Colin. She had packed foot soak powder for the Sheriff's injury, and some salve for Colin's hand. She'd made both from roots and leaves. I didn't understand why she couldn't just go to Hadley's and get a tube of Bacitracin for each of them.

And in addition to the salve, she also was packing a slew of questions for Colin. But we soon found that he wasn't at the Sheriff's office. He was going on a fishing trip for the next three days.

How do you go fishing in the middle of a murder investigation?

But of course Colin not being at the office didn't put a dent in Miss Vivee's sail. We left the healing powder for the Sheriff, and then drove to Colin's house. And I'm sure if he hadn't of been there, we would have gone on our own fishing trip to find him.

When we arrived at his house, a small white, one story, we found him loading up his black pick-up truck. He had on a pair of straight legged jeans and a light blue denim shirt that looked like it was made for him. With looks like his, I was thinking that I could look past the "he's so dumb" part. Although, the jury was still out on that one for me anyway. Who lets a man, without some level of intelligence, be a deputy? Maybe Miss Vivee over exaggerated about his lack of mental capabilities.

I was willing to take a chance. And I knew, that would make my daddy happy – me giving Colin a chance. I needed to use my energy on something other than being a good an archaeologist as my mother.

All I needed was to get up the courage to make a pass at him . . .

Once we found Colin, Miss Vivee didn't waste any time trying to get the information she needed from him. She handed him the salve at the same time she handed him her first question.

"What do you know about Gemma Burke during the time she lived in Atlanta?" she asked.

"I really can't tell you anything, Miss Vivee. It's an open investigation. The Sheriff would be really upset with me."

"I just want to know what she did when she was in Atlanta," Miss Vivee said. "How would that compromise your investigation? Especially if it was Renmar's bouillabaisse that killed her."

"Why do you want to know, anyway?" he said his eyes going from me back to Miss Vivee. "What are you two up to?" He placed fishing rods and a large white bucket in the bed of the truck. "Is this something I should tell Sheriff Haynes?"

"We're not up to anything," I said and held up my hands. "Miss Vivee was just wondering."

Miss Vivee wasn't coming up with any of her fantastical stories to tell Colin and I didn't know quite what to say. Her tactic with him appeared to be "badgering," which was a long way off from what I wanted to do with him.

"You were both up there at the same time. In Atlanta," Miss Vivee said. "You must've seen her."

"I went to Atlanta before she did," he said.

"Then did you even know she was there?" I asked. I looked at Miss Vivee. "Maybe he didn't know."

"I knew," he said putting a cooler in the truck. "I came home one weekend and found she'd sold her parents' home and left town." He turned to look at us, he stood with his feet shoulder width apart and crossed his arms. "Hadn't even known she was putting it up for sale."

"Did that make you curious about where she was?" I asked. My mouth got dry and there was pang in my stomach. Was that jealousy? About a dead girl? *Geesh.*

"A little." He gave a nod. "I must admit I was a little curious," Colin said. "I'd always thought we'd be together, you know. I'd be the deputy. Gemma would be my wife. We'd live here in Yasamee and raise our kids." He kicked rocks in his gravel driveway around with the toe of his shoe. "But now that will never happen."

"So then how did you find out she went to Atlanta?" Miss Vivee asked.

"I knew she'd have to put her address on the deed. That's what we did when my daddy died and we had to transfer the house to me. So, before I left to go back to finish my training, I went and looked up her address in the land office," he said. "I just wanted to know, you know. And lo and behold. She had gone to Atlanta. Right where I was. I thought maybe she had followed me."

"Then did you go and see her?" I was hoping he would say no.

He said, "No."

Yay!

"You mean that you were up in Atlanta and you knew she was there and you didn't look up her?" Miss Vivee seemed surprised. "Somebody from home? As far away as you were from it?"

"She had dumped me. She should have come to me."

"She didn't dump you, Colin Pritchard. You know that and everybody else in Yasamee knows it too. She didn't want to date you. All this talk about you two getting married. It's just nonsense." Colin's eyes showed dejection as he listened to Miss Vivee. "Ain't no shame in it, though," she continued. "Plenty of people ain't meant to be together. You and Gemma were just two of those people."

"Yeah. And with her rejecting me like that, you'd think I'd go and see her?"

"I sure do." Miss Vivee put one hand on her hip and held on to the side of his truck with the other. "I know you. You ain't one to give up. You must have visited her when you both were in Atlanta," Miss Vivee said. "You can't tell me, Colin Pritchard that you were in the same city as a hometown girl, one that you were crazy about and you didn't go and say 'Hello.' I can't believe you'd forget your manners like that."

He went back to saying that he couldn't just give out information in the middle of a police investigation. He had finished loading his truck and was standing by the door, ready to go. But Miss Vivee stayed on him. Finally, he bowed his head and gave in.

"I did go to see her," he said. "But . . . When I saw her . . ." he said hesitantly. "Well I was too embarrassed for her to say anything. I left and after that tried to push Gemma out of my mind. Just forget about her. I didn't want her to have to face me."

"Why?" Miss Vivee squinted one eye. "What was she doing?"

He took in a breath. "Working in a strip bar," he said and climbed inside of his truck. He rolled down the window and started his car. "And I ain't saying no more about it Miss Vivee. I felt so bad for her then, having to live that kind of life. And I feel even worse for her now that she's dead, right when she was trying to fix her life."

"Oh bother," Miss Vivee said. "Me too. I feel bad. Still . . ." She walked over, facing the car and put her hand on the door through the opened window. Leaning in, she said, "I have just *one* more question."

Chapter Twenty-One

On the ride home, Miss Vivee was quiet. I think she felt like we'd run into a dead end. She'd asked him the name of the strip club and where in Atlanta it was located, but he said initially that he couldn't remember. Miss Vivee had got its general location but no more. It seemed that Colin didn't want to gossip about Gemma's fall into disgrace.

And although I did talk to him by asking a question or two, I know I didn't do anything close to flirting. Unless he could read my mind, and saw the little fringes of jealousy that eked out when he talked about Gemma, he had no idea how I felt.

I'm just so much of a bookworm. No social skills. I looked at Miss Vivee. She was chewing her bottom lip, lost in thought. I should be more like her, I thought. Be brave. Take charge . . . Take chances.

Did I have that in me?

I shook those thoughts out of my head and exhaled loudly. Miss Vivee glanced at me and gave me a half-smile that showed her mind was preoccupied. I decided not to say anything about her "investigation" ending. I didn't want to upset her more.

"A strip club?" she said it out of the blue. We had turned the corner down her street. "Lord Almighty." She shook her head. It was the first time she'd spoke since we left Colin's.

"Unbelievable, huh?"

"Yes. Unbelievable." She let out a long breath. "Looks like we're going to Atlanta."

"What? No! We can't go to Atlanta." I turned and looked at her. This was a good a time as any to start taking charge. "Why would we go to Atlanta?" I asked.

"To investigate, Sweetie Pie." She winked her eye. "We got to find out if Gemma Burke did something to somebody up there. Enough something to make them want to come down here and kill her."

"We're going to go and find a killer?" I said. I pulled up in front of the Maypop.

"Well ain't that what we set out to do from the beginning?" She smiled and patted my arm. "You're not getting cold feet on me now are you?"

This taking charge, being bolder thing was not working with Miss Vivee. She may have had more experience at it than me, but I wasn't going to give up.

"No. I'm not getting cold feet," I said. "It's just that Atlanta is such a big place. And as you would say, it'll be like finding a needle in a haystack."

"No it's not, Sugar," she said. "Because we know just where to look."

With all this calling me "sweetie pie" and "sugar," I knew trying to win a fight with Miss Vivee over this idea of hers was going to be an uphill battle.

All I could do was pray for strength.

* * * * * *

Monday Morning, AGD

Renmar had got wind of our "alleged" trip. Only she thought that we were going to Augusta. Miss Vivee had evidently told her that she wanted to go to a movie and dinner and stay overnight at a hotel in the "big city." But instead of questioning Miss Vivee about it, Renmar decided to give me the third degree.

"What movie are you going to see . . . Which hotel are you staying in . . . Are you and mother staying in the same room?"

I had walked into the kitchen on Renmar, Brie and Hazel sitting around the large table drinking coffee. Renmar started shooting out questions before I could grab a cup. But I didn't have a chance to answer her barrage of questions before she finally threw up her hands. "I've tried talking to her," she said. "I don't know what else to do."

"Me too," Brie replied. "But she won't listen."

"To anyone," Renmar said. She took a sip of her coffee.

"I don't know about anyone," Hazel Cobb said. "She's cozied up to our little Miss Archaeologist." Hazel rubbed my back and smiled at me.

"She definitely doesn't listen to me," I said. I walked over and grabbed a mug from the cabinet and filled it up with coffee. I had already spent all my breath trying to talk her out of it.

"Have you tried to talk her out of going?" Renmar asked seemingly as if she'd heard my thoughts. "I know she has these big plans. But Augusta is twenty-five miles away. If anything happened I'd have to try and get all the way up there to see about her."

I stirred cream and sugar into my coffee and lifted it up to my mouth.

And Atlanta, I thought watching Renmar over the rim of my cup, *where she really wants to go, is one hundred forty five miles away. Surprise!*

"Why does she have to go all the way up there?" Brie asked.

"I don't know," I lied. And then I tried to explain how usually Miss Vivee doesn't tell me anything and

I just follow her directions. "Do what I'm told," I said, which was basically the truth. I also threw in that my mother had taught me to mind my manners and respect my elders, especially people as old as Miss Vivee, however old that was. With their southern gentility, I'd knew Renmar and Brie would appreciate that and stop questioning me.

"My mother has a tendency to bite off more than she can chew," Renmar said her voice softer, seemingly giving me some reprieve. "So I've told her that she can't go."

Hazel laughed. "And you think that'll work?"

"Well, she can't go if she doesn't have a ride," Renmar said and eyed me.

"Oh please." I put my cup down on the table. "Please don't put me in the middle of it," I said. "Please." I looked at Renmar, begging with my eyes. "Plus, I've already tried to talk her out of it. I don't want to feel as if I'm being disrespectful."

"Well, just try to talk her out of it, Logan. Again. For me. And if that doesn't work, I won't blame you." She threw up her hands. "How can I? If she doesn't listen to me, her own daughter, I surely can't expect her to listen to you."

"I'll try," I said. The four of us talked and sipped on coffee. Once I finished my coffee and put the mug in the sink I said, "So where is she? I've looked all over the house for her."

"She's out back. In her greenhouse. Where she used to spend all her days." Renmar looked at me, frustration in her eyes. "I didn't mean anything by that towards you. It's just that she's got the bug now. Can't sit still. Used to be I couldn't get her to go anywhere, now I can't keep her home."

I gave a "What can you do?" look and headed out the back door.

Chapter Twenty-Two

The backyard was huge. It went on for what looked like a couple of acres. In the five days I'd been staying at the Maypop, I hadn't even realized that there was a backyard, let alone something that looked like this. Miss Vivee would definitely say that that proved I had no detecting skills.

How could I have missed all of this?

There was patio area, with a fire pit, fireplace, gas grill and colorful furniture. A three car garage and carport. Flowers were everywhere, and Miss Vivee's greenhouse was the size of a small cabin. But what made it the best backyard I'd ever seen was that there was a miniature putt-putt golf course right smack dab in the middle of it.

I followed a stone path to the greenhouse and cupping my hands, I put my face up to the glass and peered in. I could see Miss Vivee inside working on her plants.

I had decided to try again to talk Miss Vivee out of going to Atlanta. Not just because Renmar had asked me to, but because I was sure that there was no way we were ever going to solve Gemma's murder, anyway. And no way, in a night club of ill-repute, were we going to find answers to who killed her, if she had even been killed.

I knocked on the door, opened it and went in. A bombardment of odors went up my nose and made my head swirl.

I could smell lavender, honeysuckle, rosemary, sage, roses, lilies and so many other things that I didn't have any idea what they were.

"Wow. Smells good in here," I said and smiled. Miss Vivee had on her rubber boots, one of her signature coats and her hair pinned up at the back of her head. Cat was resting at her feet. "So who plays golf?" I asked.

"I do," she said. She was pruning and repotting several plants she had on a workstation that she was standing in front of. "And I'm much better at it than that little putt-putt course would lead on," she said pointing her head toward it.

"Well aren't you full of surprises."

"You don't know the half of it, Missy. I've lived a long time." She eyed me. "So what you up to?"

"Nothing," I said. And walked around the tables overflowing with plants that filled the greenhouse. "Just thought I'd come and see you," I said. I touched a leaf of a purple passionflower plant and leaned over and inhaled. *Maypop*, I thought and smiled. "I didn't know you grew plants?"

"I grow some plants for healing. Some I grow for enjoyment. Without looking up, she said, "There's a lot of things that you don't know about me."

"I see," I said. "What kind of healing do you do?"

"I practice Voodoo."

"What?" I said and stopped dead in my tracks. "Unbelievable." I shook my head and starting walking around again. "A golfing, Voodoo doctor."

"Voodoo herbalist," she corrected.

I walked over to where she stood and saw cabinets that lined the wall filled with dried herbs and bottles labeled with what was inside.

"How did you learn all of this?" I asked.

"Louis Colquett. At least he got me started."

"Bay's father taught you all about this?"

"Mmm hmmm. Some of it. Louis introduced me to it although I had always used roots and plants to help those with ailments from the time I was young. When I was coming up they didn't have bottled medicines, you know. But, then, after he showed me different things, I took a trip to New Orleans." She looked over me. "I lived there for about five years. Studied under a Voodoo mambo."

"Really? I knew I should be afraid of you."

"Don't worry, Honeybun. I like you," she said grinning.

"Sooo. Can't you do some spell, or something, and divine the murderer?" I thought I may as well get to the matter at hand – talking Miss Vivee out of going to Atlanta.

"Doesn't work like that." She glanced at me. "Can't solve murders like that. At least with any powers I have. You have to deduce who the murderer is from clues."

"Oh," I said wondering how I was ever going to talk her out of looking for clues.

"So what do we know so far?" Miss Vivee asked, evidently ready to start using her powers to deduce.

"Not enough to know what killed her or who did it," I said. I went over and sat on a high stool next to where she stood."

"I already know *what* killed her."

"Are you ever going to share that with me?" I asked.

"In due time," she replied. "In due time."

I huffed. "Okay. Let's see. Suspects: Renmar Colquett." I started counting on my fingers. "Jeffery Beck. Miranda Beck. Who by the way," I noted. "We know nothing about."

"Keep going."

"Uhm, oh, the roommate, Koryn Razner." I glanced down at my finger and up to Miss Vivee. "I think that's it."

She nodded in agreement.

"And we know," I continued. "That Gemma was killed either at the park or at her house. Or anywhere past the Jellybean Café and between those two places and here, or somewhere else that could include the entire town."

I'm sure I was being too sarcastic for Miss Vivee because by the time I finished she had a scowl on her face.

"Renmar thinks I shouldn't take you to Atlanta, although *she* thinks we're going to Augusta." I said deciding to just come out with it. "She said she's going to have to put her foot down and insist that you don't go."

Miss Vivee lifted an eyebrow. "Did she now?"

"Yep. She did." I got up and walked to her shelf of herbs and picked up a bottle filled with a pretty sparkling orange powder. "So, I'm thinking that we won't be going to Atlanta and checking out that strip bar."

"Be careful with that. It could kill you."

I put the bottle with the pretty sparkling orange powder back on the shelf – gingerly.

"She also said that you always bite off more than you can chew. So translating that into terms of solving this thing about Gemma – well, I was thinking, it might be a bit much for you. I'm sure she would say that, besides the fact, we're not supposed to be doing it. Renmar told me that all of this going out is just too much for you."

That last part may not have been what she said, exactly, but I had to try.

"Well, aren't you the little instigator?" Miss Vivee said.

"Me?" I frowned my brow. *This little plan seemed to be backfiring.* "I'm not instigating. I'm just telling you what she said." I went back and sat on the stool, and fiddled with some dirt that was scattered on her workstation. "And I think maybe she's right. We haven't gotten the autopsy report back yet and we've hit a snag with finding out that it may be someone in Atlanta that committed the crime." I looked at her out the side of my eyes. "*If* a crime was committed."

"Gemma Burke was murdered. Mark my words on that. And that's what that autopsy report will read when it gets back." She seemed to be working up an anger. "And I don't care what Renmar thinks about me. I *can* figure this thing out. And I *will* figure it out. I'm not feeble minded you know. I do my crossword puzzles, Sudoku and all those little brain exercises to keep my mind sharp." She tightened her lips. "Not that I need to."

I hadn't meant to upset her. *Maybe*, I thought, *I should make her understand what I mean.*

"She didn't say -" I started.

"I don't care what she said," Miss Vivee interrupted me, hissing out the words. "I know what I saw. I know what happened to that girl."

"Well, that may be all that we'll ever be able to know about it," I said. "You certainly can't go to Atlanta and find out anything. It's too far and you wouldn't know where to start."

"You listen here, Missy." She gripped her pruning shears a little tighter and pointed them at me. "Don't tell me what I can and can't do. I was grown before you were a twinkle in your daddy's eye. Hell, before *he* was a twinkle in *his* daddy's eye." She threw the shears on her table and started pounding on the dirt that surrounded the plant. "I'll go to Atlanta if I want to. You best believe that. And pay no mind to what Renmar says . . . or thinks. She don't know jack about what I'm capable of. She thinks I didn't kill her husband."

My eyes got big. "You killed her husband?"

Vivee's face went from anger, to surprise, to sheepish. "Don't you ever say a word to anyone," she let out in a squeak. "I'll deny I ever said that. Not a word." She pointed her finger at me. "You hear me? I know how you like to stir up trouble."

I laughed. "No I don't like to 'stir' up trouble."

"I ain't so sure." She sang the words.

"I won't say anything to anyone. I promise. But you did say it," I said. "You said you killed Renmar's husband."

"I guess I let that cat outta the bag, huh?"

"Does that mean you killed her husband?"

Miss Vivee bowed her head and closed her eyes. She was quiet for a long moment.

"Not exactly" she finally said after a long sigh. "And not mostly."

"But?" I held out my hands questioningly. She bit her bottom lip. "What, Miss Vivee? What in the world does 'not mostly' mean?"

"Means that the 'most' part of him dying I had nothing to do with."

"You have to tell me what you mean."

"Only if you take me to Atlanta."

Chapter Twenty-Three

Monday Afternoon, AGD

"We just can't go to a strip club alone," I said. I had given up trying to talk her out of it.

"Why not?"

"Look at us. An old woman and an archaeologist. We don't fit."

I was sitting on Miss Vivee's bed watching her as she pulled out dress after dress trying to decide what to wear. Her hair was loose and hung down her back and she was all smiles. She acted like she was going on her first date, no outfit seemed to be the right one. I wondered did she actually think she could find something in her closet that would be just the right thing for a hundred-year old woman to wear to a strip club.

Cat on the other hand liked everything she had pulled out. She barked her approval of each choice.

Miss Vivee's room was big and filled with antiques. When you walked through her bedroom door it was like stepping back in time. She had a big, four-poster bed, floor and table lamps with fringe hanging from the bottom of them, dark wine-colored wallpaper, and a beautiful mahogany wood vanity with a silk covered stool. And there were pictures of Bay all over.

I wouldn't have been able to stomach all the "*Bay-ness*" if she hadn't been holding information that I wanted over my head. The only way, she had told me, that I was going to find out what she had to do with Louis Colquett's death was if I took her to Atlanta. And to be sure I didn't renege on my part, she told me she would only tell me once we got back. Plus, after I realized how much it meant to her, I didn't have the heart not to take her. What's a trip two hours up the road? So I was stuck going to a strip club in Atlanta, and suffering through the "Eyes of Bay" staring at me from every corner of the room.

"I see what you mean," she said and sat down on the bed next to me. "Just the two of us can't go. We need to take a man with us. Make us look more legit." she said and bit down on her lip.

Legit? Where did she get that word from?

"We could ask Bay to go with us," she said, a questioning look on her face.

"No," I practically shouted out the words. She raised her eyebrows at my outburst. "It's just . . . you know . . . He won't let you investigate like you want," I said. I didn't want her to know that I was afraid if I was anywhere near that man he would trick me into confessing my crimes. I tried to steer clear of him at all cost.

"That's true," she said thoughtfully. "I've got it," she said, snapping her finger. She hopped up and Cat jumped with her, tail wagging on "high." She grabbed both my hands. "We'll ask Mac!"

I thought she was going to pull me up and start dancing she was so elated over her decision.

"Who?" I asked.

"He'll be our cover," she said beaming. Then we'll look like we belong."

"Who?" I asked again. Then it hit me. "You mean the ninety-year old man that was at the diner staring at you? That Mac?"

"Yes. That Mac. I only know one Mac. I'll call him and tell him to meet us at the diner. We can tell him our plans." She stopped and squinted her eyes. "I would go to his house, but I vowed I never step foot in there again." She shook her shoulders and looked at me. "That'll work fine. The diner. We'll meet him at the diner."

I wasn't as enthused about Mac as she was.

"I really don't think taking an ol- I mean him — Mac will help us."

"Why not? Don't be silly."

"He may not want to go. Or be up to it." I remembered how upset Miss Vivee got the last time we ran into him. I just didn't think it would be a good idea for her to be like that all the way to Atlanta and back.

"Oh hogwash," she said. "That man'll do anything I ask him. He's in love with me you know."

I arched an eyebrow. "No. I didn't know." That comment nipped my concern in the bud. "Soooo," I started slowly. "Do you love him?"

"Of course I do."

I smiled. *How cute.*

"Then why aren't you together. And why did you barely speak to him when we saw him at the diner? And why did you duck down in the seat when we passed his house?"

"You ask a lot of questions, Missy."

"I'm a scientist."

"Poohey."

I laughed. "So what's the answer?"

"To which question?"

"All of them, Miss Vivee. Spill the beans."

She lowered her eyes and came back to sit on the bed with me. "I'm mad at him."

"What happened?"

She took in a breath. She glanced at me and then stared down at her hands that she had folded in her lap.

"I ran him over with my car," she said in a low, contrite voice.

"Oh?" That's the only thing I could think to say.

"You know that little limp he has when he walks?" she asked. I nodded my head. "It's because of me and my brand new 1994 Lincoln Continental. I call her Betsy – she's a great car. Anyway, we broke his hip."

"Wait. 1994? That was like twenty years ago."

She nodded.

"You two were in your seventies."

She nodded again.

"You hit a seventy year old man with your car?"

No nod this time, she just sighed and closed her eyes.

"Why?"

"I thought he was cheating on me."

I couldn't hold my laughter in any longer. "With who?"

"This hussy that lived the next street over from him," she said, her whole demeanor changing. "Ooowee! I couldn't stand her. Always smiling at him. Falling all over herself when she was around him. Cooking him dinner and inviting herself to have meals with him." Vivee waved her hand in the air. "Just the thought of it, even now, turns my stomach."

"You said you 'thought' he was. Did you find out if he really was cheating on you with her?"

"Well." She fluttered her eyes. "He said he wasn't. But you know men, if their lips are moving they're probably lying."

"So are they together now?"

"Oh God no. Don't be silly. If they were I wouldn't be taking him to Atlanta with us. She's dead and buried. Rotting in hell I hope." She turned and looked at me, the fire of her eagerness popping back into her eyes. "So Mac gets a reprieve." She clapped her hands together.

"Now come on, Missy. Get a move on." She patted me on my leg and stood up. "We gotta go and tell him about our little trip. With that limp he don't get around as quick as he used to. It'll take him some time to get ready."

Chapter Twenty-Four

Tuesday Afternoon, AGD

"Mac is here, Miss Vivee," Viola Rose whispered it as soon as we walked through the door of the Jellybean Cafe. She nodded her head toward the back of the diner. "Says he's here waiting for you, wouldn't even order anything until you got here. Wasn't sure how you felt about talking to him. I know how he dills your pickles. Maybe you'd want to come back later?"

"It's okay, Viola Rose," Miss Vivee replied. "I asked him to meet me here."

"Oh. I see," she said, drawing out the words and then flashing a conspiratorial smile.

"No. You don't see, Viola Rose. It's just business," Miss Vivee held her head up, chin jutted out and seemed to saunter toward the booth where Mac sat. "Just bring us three glasses of iced tea over, will ya?" she said over her shoulder.

She was putting on a show. I grinned. Mac sure did do something to her. After all that talk it had taken her the rest of the day to get up the nerve to call Mac and tell him to meet us at the diner. And all morning she fussed with another wardrobe dilemma. This time what to wear to see Mac. She had put on face powder and that same lipstick she'd worn for her "coming out." She had checked several times in her compact mirror on our way to the diner that everything had stayed in place. She'd even left Cat at home.

"Sure thing," Viola Rose called out to her. I turned my head to look at Viola Rose and she gave me a crooked smile.

I had promised myself I wouldn't tease, so I kept a straight face and followed behind Miss Vivee.

As we walked up to the booth, Mac stood up and waited for us to sit before he pushed himself back in on his side of the booth. I noted he didn't have his cane again.

"I ordered you an iced tea, Mac. You still drink those, don't you?" Even Miss Vivee's voice changed around Mac. It was softer and gentler.

"I do." He smiled. "Thank you."

She eyed him, and a smile crept up her lips. "What's that you got on your hair," Miss Vivee said crinkling her nose. "Looks like a cow licked it."

His hand immediately shot up to it head and he swiped a hand across it. He had his all white hair parted on the side and slicked down.

"Pomade," he answered.

Miss Vivee raised her eyebrows and said, "Hmmmm."

Okay, so maybe it was just her voice that was nicer, because her attitude hadn't changed.

Mac looked as his hand, the one he had swiped across the pomade, and then wiped it on a napkin he got out of the holder.

Viola Rose brought the drinks over, she had a coke for me instead of iced tea. *How nice she remembered.* She sat them down in front of us. "Anything else," she asked.

"Not now, Viola Rose," Miss Vivee dismissed her with a wave. "I'll let you know if we change our minds."

I leaned into Miss Vivee. "Maybe he wanted something to eat." I nodded my head toward Mac.

"Who? Mac?" Miss Vivee looked at me and then over at Mac. "Did you want something to eat, Mac?"

I saw a glint in his eye and almost a smile cross his face. "No Vivee. I'll wait for you."

She gave me a "That's what I thought look," then jumped like she'd been startled. "Oh my," she said sitting up straight in her seat. "Where are my

165

manners?" She pointed to me. "Logan Dickerson this is Macomber Whitson. Mac, this is my good friend and companion, Logan."

"Pleasure to meet you," I said wondering when Miss Vivee and I had become "good friends."

"Just call me, Mac," he said and stuck out his hand for me to shake.

"Mac is a doctor," Miss Vivee said to me with a nod. "Tell her, Mac."

"I'm a doctor," he said as instructed.

"Same kind of, um, doctor as you?" I said. I had to refrain from putting air quotes around the word "doctor."

"I told you, I'm an herbalist. So. No," she said. "He went to school. Graduated top of his class. Didn't you, Mac?"

"Yes. I did." He seemed to blush. I guess he liked Miss Vivee bragging about him.

"He was the town doctor. Birthed most of the people in this town and took care of them while they grew up, got old and died." She stared right at Mac as she talked. "Back then the town wasn't as big as it is now."

All five hundred people big, I thought.

She broke her stare and looked at me. "Are you hungry?"

"Me?" *Oh, did she care?* "No. I'll wait for you," I said. I figured Mac's answer had been the right one.

"So," Miss Vivee said and hesitated, leaving an awkward silence among us. She seemed unsure of what she wanted to say or at least how she wanted to say it. The plan was to get him to go to Atlanta with us.

Had she changed her mind?

She licked her lips and then took a sip of her iced tea. "Mac," she finally said. "You heard about Gemma Burke?"

"Sure did. Terrible thing. Word going around it was Renmar's bouillabaisse that killed her."

"Well that's a lie," Miss Vivee said adamantly.

"How do *you* think she died, Vivee?" he asked, the question etched in his face.

He knew her well. Right away he knew she thought something else was going on.

Miss Vivee looked at me and then leaned across the table. Mac leaned in as well.

"I think she was murdered," Miss Vivee whispered.

Mac sat back slowly. I wasn't sure if because he was surprised about Miss Vivee's revelation or because that's all the fast he could move.

"Well now," he said and wiped his mouth with his napkin. "And who do you think did the murdering?"

Before Miss Vivee could answer, Viola Rose popped back over. "Just checking back for food orders." She stood poised with order pad and pen.

"Maybe in a minute, Viola Rose," Miss Vivee said visibly annoyed with her. And then we all sat quietly. No one speaking as long as she stood there.

Viola Rose looked around the table, clicked the top of her pen a few times and said, "Well I guess I can take a hint." She clicked the pen once more stuck it through her teased hair and put the order pad in her pocket. "Just give me a holler if you decide you want anything."

As she walked off, Miss Vivee said, "Hadn't I already told her that I would?"

I laughed. But Mac picked the conversation back up. He seemed keen to hear what Miss Vivee had to say.

"So, Vivee," Mac said. "Who's the murderer?" He eyed her. "Do you know?"

"Not yet. But I've been doing some investigating and I've got a list of suspects."

"Really now. And who's on the list?"

She looked at me and back at him. "It's incomplete right now. But we're on the trail of a couple of them."

He nodded his head slowly, and let his eyes drift upward. He seemed to contemplate Miss Vivee's theory of murder.

"So since you know that she was murdered, you must know *how* she was murdered," he said bringing his eyes down to meet hers.

"I do," she said and took a sip of her tea.

My ears perked up. She had yet to share her thoughts of how Gemma Burke was murdered with me. It seemed as if she felt like I should just have blind faith in her and follow her every command, without question, as she carried through on her inquisition.

I chuckled. *And that was exactly what I had been doing.*

Chapter Twenty-Five

I don't know if Miss Vivee's pregnant pause was for a dramatic effect or if she had lost her train of thought. But it took her a few minutes to fill us in on how she thought Gemma had been killed. The silence was killing me.

"When Gemma came into the Maypop she was coughing," Miss Vivee finally said. "She couldn't seem to catch her breath. Her face looked distressed and she complained to Renmar of chest pains and that she felt really tired."

"Wait," I said. "You told me she bounced in. Ponytail swinging. This is the first I've heard that she was sick when she came in."

"I used the word 'bouncy' metaphorically," she explained. "You know, to show the contrast in her state of being in a short amount of time – alive when she came in and dead when she left," she explained.

I rolled my eyes.

"Anyway." Miss Vivee directed her attention back to Mac. "She had on one of those running suits."

"Sweats," I offered.

"No. She wasn't sweating," Miss Vivee said. "You weren't there. You didn't see her." She looked at Mac. "She didn't see her."

"No. I meant her outfit. We call them sweats."

"Oh. Okay. I didn't want Mac to think that sweating was one of the symptoms, because it wasn't." Miss Vivee took a sip of her tea. "Anyway. She coughed the entire time she was there until she fell over dead in her bowl of bouillabaisse. And her 'sweats' were dirty, like she'd been on the ground."

A knowing smile crossed Mac's face and his eyes lit up. "Like she had had a fall?"

"Exactly." Miss Vivee's eyes gleamed.

"You think she dry drowned, don't you?" he said.

Miss Vivee practically leapt up in her seat. Then she turned and grabbed my arm and squeezed it. "See? He agrees," she said to me. "Mac thinks the same thing I do. Gemma Burke was murdered."

"Wait! What?" I was totally confused.

"Vivee thinks Gemma dry drowned."

"In the bouillabaisse?"

"No." Miss Vivee frowned up her face. "Not in the bouillabaisse," she said with some frustration in her voice. "Are you always this slow?"

I opened my mouth to talk and then thought better of it.

"Tell her, Mac," Miss Vivee ordered.

"From what Vivee tells me, I'd have to concur. I think she dry drowned." He scooted up closer to the table. "You see people drown when their lungs can't get enough oxygen from the air. Normally a person drowns because of some kind of fluid in the lungs. But dry drowning is when a person can't pull in enough oxygen for some reason other than the presence of a liquid."

"Isn't that the same as suffocation?" I asked.

Miss Vivee clucked her teeth.

"It's the cause and effect," Mac offered. "Gemma suffocated yes, but the reason was because she drowned."

"The *no* water drowning," Miss Vivee said. "So it's called *dry* drowning."

I looked over at Miss Vivee and back at Mac. I had never heard of dry drowning before. I was so tempted to pull out my iPhone and Google it. But that would upset Miss Vivee that I had to confirm what she and Mac were telling me. I made a mental note to look it up later. In the privacy of my room.

"How do you two know that?" I said instead.

"The symptoms of course," Miss Vivee said. "She came in coughing. When she sat down to eat she told Renmar that she thought some of her soup would help her. And she had dirt on her clothes."

"Coughing?" I said. "That's all?" I shook my head in disbelief.

"And the dirt on her clothes," Miss Vivee said.

"You could tell from that?" I said confused. "That's what made you know she dry drowned. Or whatever it's called. Maybe she just swallowed the wrong way, or she was catching a cold."

"You don't die from a cold. Or from swallowing the wrong way. Leastways not that quickly. And you don't cough that long." Miss Vivee didn't like the idea that I wasn't just falling in line with her coughing culprit version of Gemma's death.

"Vivee said that Gemma complained to Renmar of being tired. Having chest pain," Mac said.

"I heard Renmar tell the Sheriff that," Miss Vivee said and gave a quick nod of her head. "And Brie confirmed it."

Mac looked at me. "I know it seems quite incredulous for us to make that assumption on so little information. And you're right, there's lots of things that'll make you cough. But there aren't many things that will make you cough and kill you." He nodded his head slowly. "Go ahead. Gaggle it," he said and sat back in his seat, seemingly quite pleased with himself.

"Gaggle it?" I crunched up my nose.

"You know," Miss Vivee said. "On the World Wide Web."

I started laughing. I had planned to later on, but since they were okay with it, I whipped out my phone.

"Just do a search for coughing as a symptom," he said.

And while I searched, I heard Miss Vivee talk to Mac about what she had come to ask.

"Mac," she said. "Like I said, we're on the trail of a few of the suspects. And it's led us to a strip club in Atlanta."

"Really?"

"Yes. And . . . Well. Logan and I, upstanding women that we are, can't go into one of those places by ourselves."

"So you and Logan are solving the murder?"

"Logan's an archaeologist," Miss Vivee said.

I glanced up when she said that. I wondered was being an archaeologist a step up or down from me being "a good friend and companion."

"And she knows all about solving murders," Miss Vivee continued, her voice was so sweet it could have sweeten a whole sea of iced tea.

"And?" he asked. He seemed eager to find out what she wanted.

"Well." I saw her lick her lips out the side of my eye. "I want you to ride to Atlanta with us," she said, rather meekly for her. "You know. For protection and to help with our investigation."

He smiled. "When you thinking about leaving?"

"Tomorrow," she said and smiled.

"I'm in," he said returning the smile.

"Thank you, Mac," she said. She batted what was left of her eyelashes and blushed. "I knew I could count on you." Then in the same breath, the smile disappeared and she raised an eyebrow. "And when we go," her voice dropped an octave lower. "Don't wear any of that pomade."

She patted her hands on the table and said, "Now, we're all set." She nodded her head at me. "I'm going to the little's girl's room. You need to go?"

"No. I'm good," I muttered barely looking up from my phone. There really was a thing called dry drowning. I Googled "cough symptom" and every illness it listed wasn't very serious or took a really long time like emphysema or lung cancer. Except for dry drowning. It took anywhere from one to twenty-four hours to kill a person. The symptoms, according to WebMD were coughing, chest pain and shortness of breath.

Wow. Maybe Miss Vivee really did know what she was talking about.

Once she left, Mac slid down his bench so he was directly across from me. "I know Vivee must've told you that story about me, her and Betsy."

"Huh," I said and looked up from my phone. "Betsy?" the name sounded familiar.

"Her car. My limp." He pointed down to his leg.

"Oh yeah," I said realizing what he was talking about. "She told me." My face cringed remembering the incident.

"Well. I'm sure she made it sound a lot worse than it was."

"Oh?" I said, my mouth lingering in the shape of the letter "O."

Was he getting ready to defend her for hitting him with her car? Oh my goodness. He couldn't be.

"She said she ran you over with her car and broke your hip," I said slowly then waited to hear his answer.

"See. That's what I mean. She didn't *run* me over, she just kind of bumped me with it. I could have moved out the way, but I didn't really believe her when she said she was 'gonna mow me down.'"

I just closed my eyes and shook my head.

"And she didn't *break* my hip," he continued. "It was just fractured." He rearranged the silverware in front of him. He seemed to be thinking over what he wanted to say.

"I wasn't messing with that woman, you know. 'The Hussy,' as Vivee calls her," he said sounding like he wanted me to believe him. "*She* was messin' with me. I told her I didn't want no parts of her or her cooking."

"Miss Vivee told me she's dead now."

He looked at me, curiosity flashing across his face. "She didn't tell you she killed her, did she?"

"*Did* she kill her?" I said a little louder than he liked.

"Shhh!" He reached over the table and squeezed my wrist. "Don't talk so loud," he said and scanned the room checking to see if anyone had heard me. He let me go, took a sip of his iced tea and cleared his throat.

"Nobody's saying she killed her," he said, almost fussing at me. "But the woman died not too long after the incident with the car." He glanced at me and then fiddled with the straw in his glass. "I just always wondered if it was Vivee . . . The coroner up in Augusta said it was a heart attack. But you know Vivee with her herbs and concoctions . . . She could make it seem like a heart attack."

"I'm learning a lot about her capabilities," I said and took a sip of my pop. "No wonder she's so interested in finding Gemma's killer. They're two of a kind." I said low, almost muttering.

"I'm back!" Miss Vivee came waltzing, well as much as she could at ninety-something, back over to the table and slid into the booth next to me. Happiness oozing out of her.

"What you two got your heads together about?" she said all smiles.

"Nothing," we said in unison.

She looked at the two of us. "Well good. Now. Did anyone order anything? I'm starving."

Chapter Twenty-Six
Interstate Route 20, North

Wednesday Afternoon, AGD

"What's in the bag, Miss Vivee?"

We were in Miss Vivee's car, the 1994, gas guzzling, "Mow Your Man Down" Lincoln Towncar, on our way to Atlanta. She had refused to go in my Jeep Wrangler saying she didn't want to ride for hours on end that high up. Plus, she had said, she would wrinkle her dress climbing in and out of it. She acted as if we were going on a road trip across the country. So I was stuck driving the weapon she'd used to assault and maim Dr. Mac Whitson.

"Our lunch," she said and shook the bag at me.

"Lunch? There's plenty of places on the way to eat," I said.

"And spend good money buying food when there's perfectly good food at the house that we can take with us? Nonsense."

"What do you have?" Mac asked. He had come over to the Maypop before we left. Miss Vivee refused to go to his house to pick him up. She wouldn't even let me leave by myself and go and get him.

"If he wants to go, he can get here on his own," she had said. She must've forgotten she'd asked him to go. I knew, though, it was all because of the vow she made never to set foot in his house again.

"I packed egg salad," Miss Vivee said to Mac. "Viola Rose heard about my trip and brought me over a whole tub of it. I brought goose liver for you and Logan." She pulled out a waxed paper wrapped bundle and waved it in the air. "I put it both on white and wheat bread. You can take your pick."

I stuck out my tongue. "Yuck."

"You don't like goose liver?" she asked.

"No. I. Don't."

"I do," Mac said from the backseat. "Hand me one of those."

I took it from Miss Vivee and handed it over the seat to Mac.

"So, Vivee," Mac spoke with a chuck of goose liver in his jaw. "Have you come up with a theory on who killed Gemma and why?"

"I'm thinking that it was one of the Becks that killed her," Miss Vivee said.

"Who are they?" Mac asked.

"We found a letter," I offered. "It was from a man named Jeffrey Beck to Gemma. In it he said he'd be willing to leave his wife, Miranda, if Gemma would take him back. Evidently she had broken it off with him."

"Ah," he said. "A love triangle. Always a good motive." I watched in the review mirror as he shoved the rest of the sandwich in his mouth and then asked, mouth full, "Got another sandwich up there?"

"You can have mine," I said and handed him the neatly wrapped package.

"Either a love triangle with both the husband and wife involved," Miss Vivee explained to Mac. "Or maybe it was just Jeffrey Beck who killed Gemma Burke in a jealous rage."

"Maybe he killed her because she was a stripper," Mac offered.

"Who kills people because they strip?" Miss Vivee's voice had gone up an octave. "Being a stripper is like any other job – archaeologist, cook." Miss Vivee unwrapped the sandwich she'd made from the egg salad Viola Rose had given her. "You don't go around people killing people just 'cause they work in a diner do you?"

"It was just a suggestion," Mac said.

"I was a stripper once," Vivee said matter-of-factly, taking a small bite of her sandwich.

"You were not," I said.

"I could have been. Times were hard trying to raise my girls after their daddy died. I had a friend that owned a juke joint down in the swamps. And I worked there for a good little piece. Dancing. Had to smile at the customers, keep'em happy, you know. And believe me when I tell you, some of them got right friendly at times."

"Wish I'd a known you back then," Mac said.

"That's not the same as a stripper." Neither one of us paid attention to Mac's comment.

"Almost," she said. "It almost made me a stripper. Sometimes I felt like I was."

"You can strip for me anytime, Vivee," Mac said, a sly grin working its way across his wrinkled face.

"Then I won't be the blame for just your broke hip, but for that heart attack you'd have," she said over her shoulder. "You can't handle what I've got to offer, you old goat."

"At least I'd die with a smile on my face."

I took my hands off the wheel and covered my ears. "Please you two. I can't take any more."

"He started it," Miss Vivee said. "I was trying to have a civilized and proper, mind you, conversation about being a stripper."

Chapter Twenty-Seven
Atlanta, Georgia

Wednesday Night, AGD

Colin Pritchard had sworn to Miss Vivee that all he remembered about the club where Gemma had worked was its general location. Not its name. Not what it looked like. Not even which side of the street it was on.

I was beginning to see what Miss Vivee meant about him not being so smart.

He seemed hurt about Gemma spurning him, so finally confronting her should have been a big deal. Especially when he saw her in her stripper costume. Something like that should be etched in his memory. Forever. Something he'd share over a beer with friends when they talk about the one that got away.

Once we arrived, we found that there was a whole row of stripper clubs on Piedmont Avenue south of

Main – the directions he'd given us – which presented a dilemma: In which one had Gemma Burke worked?

Miss Vivee checked her notebook twice, reading and rereading from the notes she had scribbled down once we got back from speaking with Colin. She was hoping to find something more specific he'd said about where Gemma worked. Because here we were and with the number of clubs – Nipp-o-lopolis, Kitty City, and Dancing Bare, just to name a few – it looked like we were going to have to go bar hopping the rest of the night. It made me regret agreeing to come to Atlanta. And with names like those I didn't care to find out which one Gemma had worked in. I was ready to turn around and head back to Yasamee.

Mac, on the other hand, was keen on not wasting any time determining Gemma's employer. He suggested that he would go into each one of them first, alone, and do some reconnaissance. Miss Vivee gave him the evil eye and then told me to park the car, we were all going in.

I would have voted for Mac to do the honors and then come back and share any info he had gleaned. But unfortunately for me, Miss Vivee's world was not a democracy.

We tried Club Kitty City first. I found a handicap spot (go figure) right in front, we hooked the handicap sticker around the rearview mirror and headed in.

Red and purple strobe lights and half naked girls were everywhere. The club's atmosphere had to be meant to mesmerize and tantalize its clients. It put Mac in a trance. He walked in, lost his limp, and sprung a grin that lasted the entire time we were there. He had worn a gray suit that looked at least thirty years old. It had narrow pinstripes, which he complimented with a white shirt and a brown polka dot bow tie. Minus the pomade, he still tried to control that shock of white hair that framed his face by constantly rubbing it down with his hand.

The place had all the glimmer and ritz of the Las Vegas strip. There was a stage, no higher than the back of the chairs, along the back wall. It had a teak colored base, a sleek black walkway, and shiny silver stripper poles every few feet. Behind it was a backdrop that was electric. It was punctured with small holes that had red and purple lights piped through. The floor was filled with small, round tables each surrounded by three tan-colored leather upholstered, tub chairs that swiveled giving its occupants full view of all the happenings going on. And every inch of that place was crawling with "happenings." Pendant lamps gave low lighting. And those strobes swept the room on a constant pendulum bouncing to the music and off the gyrating girls.

"Now what do we do?" I asked over the loud music.

"We mingle," Miss Vivee said. "Come on, Mac." She grabbed his arm and escorted him over to the bar. I knew I'd better follow.

Miss Vivee had worn a rose pink, 1920s style flapper dress. I'm sure it wasn't from the original era, but it looked the part. She had her hair in a bun on top of her head, and flats on her feet with a strap across her instep. And, of course, her pink lipstick.

Mac easily slid onto one of the stools, but Miss Vivee, with her short frame and even shorter legs, struggled getting on one. It was just like when she tried to get into my Jeep.

"You want me to help you?" I offered.

"No," she said and groaned. Giving up, she straightened out her dress and pointed to a table. "Maybe we should just sit over there."

As the three of us walked over to the table, our eyes lit up in wonderment as the innuendos of sex swirled around us. I thought about how many of these strip joints we'd have to go into before we'd find the one where Gemma worked.

This was going to be a long night.

"Oooo. I want one of those," Miss Vivee leaned into me and said. She pointed her bony, gnarled finger at a drink a waitress dressed in a gold sequenced "string bikini" carried on a tray. It was skimpy, sparkly and clung to her like it a second skin – the bikini, not the drink. The drink was pretty and pink.

Miss Vivee tapped the waitress as she walked by. "Come back, Sweetie. After you deliver those."

The girl nodded. "Be right with ya," she said.

Didn't Ms. Sparkly Thang think it strange that a woman clearly over the three quarter century mark was ordering a drink? Or for that matter that a couple, older than dirt, were in a strip bar?

No one had even given us a second glance.

What is the world coming to?

Sparkles came back to the table all smiles, no questioning look in her eye. "What can I get y'all?"

"I want one of those drinks that you took to that lady over there sitting with all those fellows," Miss Vivee instructed. "What was that?"

"A Pink Paloma."

"That's what I'll have," she sucked on her bottom lip and made a smacking sound.

"It's got a shot of tequila in it." Sparkles seemed to want to make sure Miss Vivee knew what she was ordering.

Finally someone noticing the geriatric customers in the room.

"That's fine," Miss Vivee flashed her a sickly sweet smile. Then, "Mac," she said and elbowed him. "Order a drink."

He looked up at the waitress, he pursed his lips and squinted his eyes. "Let's see," he said and ran his hand over his wiry white hair. She's having tequila? Then so will I," he said with decisiveness. "Bring me an El Diablo,"

"Okay. And you?" Sparkles turned to me.

"I'm driving," I said and waved my hands. It would have been nice to have a drink to help cope with this scene, but I knew I had to stay sober. I was envisioning that I might have to carry both Miss Vivee and Mac to the car after they consumed just a couple of sips.

"You're not drinking, dear?" Miss Vivee asked me.

I just rolled my eyes and shook my head.

"Okay then, Sweetie," Miss Vivee said to the waitress. "That'll be it."

"What now?" I asked after Sparkles left. "What do we do now?"

"We ask questions."

"I don't think people in this kind of place are prone to answering questions from strangers."

"We'll just have to try and see," Miss Vivee said.

Sparkles came back with the drinks.

As she put them down with a napkin, Miss Vivee gently touched her hand. "We're looking for Gemma Burke. Is she here tonight? We're her grandparents." Lies rolled off of Miss Vivee's tongue just as smooth as silk.

"Gemma?"

"Yes, she goes by the name D'lishus, I believe," Miss Vivee said.

And Mac was right in there with her. "We're getting on in age and trying to get all our affairs together. It won't be long for us," he said nodding. "And we want to make sure she gets what we leave for her." He smiled at Ms. Vivee and grabbed her hand as if they were together.

"Oh. Gemma," Sparkles said. "Yeah. She did go by D'lishus. I remember her. She doesn't work here anymore. But you'd want to talk to Champagne or Buns. They were real good friends with her. They might know where she is."

I didn't know asking "questions" included making up gigantic fibs, but I was thanking the Lord we wouldn't have to go in another strip bar to find answers for Miss Vivee.

"Buns?" Mac said and looked around the room.

"Uh-huh. Buns Galore. They're both here. I'll see if I can't find one of them."

"Buns Galore," Mac leaned into the table and lowered his voice. I swear I saw a spark in that old man's eye.

"Miss Vivee," I spoke over the music. "What about if they know that Gemma is dead?"

"Oh, *pshaw*. How would they know? The girl is barely cold. And who in Yasamee would call up to a strip club to announce that Gemma Burke keeled over dead in a bowl of bouillabaisse."

"Probably no one," Mac said fiddling with his drink.

"No one," she confirmed. "We'll be fine. You'll see. Just follow my lead."

"I'm going to the restroom," I announced. "Don't do anything until I get back."

"Don't be too long," Miss Vivee said. "We can't wait if Buns and Whiskey come over. We'll have to start in on the interrogation."

"Champagne," Mac offered the correction.

"Right. Champagne. We've got to play out this storyline."

"Play out the storyline?" I scrunched up my nose. *Please Lord, give me strength.*

I made it to the restroom without having to run into too many scantily clad women and could have sat on that cold stool the entire time Miss Vivee and Mac's story "played" out. But I knew Miss Vivee needed me, even if she didn't know it. While I washed my hands, I glanced in the mirror. Shaking some of the water off, I ran my hands over my hair.

I guess I could try to do a little better with my appearance. I hadn't nearly taken the time or care Miss Vivee had when I was trying to decide what to wear, seeing my choice was very limited. I hadn't packed much. I turned my body from side to side and looked at my butt, lifted up my breast in my bra, and smoothed my hand down the yellow flower-filled sundress I had on. I ran my hand over my face and licked my lips.

Maybe a little lip gloss.

Digging down in my purse, I found two tubes of gloss. Bobbi Brown Hot Pink or Bellini High Shimmer?

Everyone else out there was glittery and shimmery, so what the heck. I dabbed some of the Bellini on my lips and found a comb. I tried to pull it through my hair. The humidity of the Georgia coast had seemed to put a permanent curl in it. I was starting to look more and more like my mother. Ugh.

I took another look at myself in the mirror and sighed. Trying to look better now, with all those beautiful, alluring women out there made my efforts seem pointless.

I headed back out to the table when a hand grabbed my arm from behind and startled me. I turned around and my eyes met a man's chest. But before I even let them trail up to his face I knew who it was.

Bay Colquett.

Oh crap.

Chapter Twenty-Eight

Bay pulled me close into him, leaning down, he whispered breathily in my ear through my hair. "I like that lipstick," he said. I could feel the heat from his words on my neck. I didn't know what he was trying to do, but whatever it was, it was making me nervous.

"T-Thank you," I said, stumbling over my words.

Then he pushed me back. That stupid smirk of his appearing over his face. "Don't make me have to arrest you, Dr. Dickerson" he said. "I'd hate to throw you in jail while you're looking so pretty."

"Arrest me for what?"

Why is he always picking on me?

"Contributing to the delinquency of the elderly," he said and pointed over toward Miss Vivee and Mac sitting at the table sipping on their drinks.

I turned and looked. The sight of those two made me chuckle. "It's more like they're contributing to the delinquency of me."

He raised an eyebrow.

"You think I frequent strip bars? Or even bars for that matter."

"Until you came to Yasamee my grandmother hadn't left the house in more than twenty years."

"So I've heard." I glanced again at the two of them. Miss Vivee was deep in conversation with one of the strippers they had yoked into talking to them. "Trust me when I tell you," I said. "The world was a safer place when she was inside."

"C'mon outside with me. I want to have a talk with you."

"About what?" I said not moving. "Can't we just talk in here?"

He tugged at my arm. "C'mon."

"Really. I need to go and check on Miss Vivee," I tried to yell over the music as he dragged me across the floor and out the door. "Your mother told me to watch her," I said in a huff.

"My mother doesn't even know you're here," he said after he got me outside. "She thinks you're in Augusta."

I took in a sharp breath. "Look. It's hard to lie to your mother, but it's much harder to breach my allegiance to your grandmother."

"I know," he said.

He was staring at me, his hazel eyes bewitching. I suddenly felt uneasy – shy – embarrassed. And self-conscious.

Did I have something on my nose? Around my mouth.

"How did you know we were here, anyway?" I said and started swiping at my face to remove anything stuck on it.

"Grandmother told me. And I saw that big monstrosity she calls a car parked in front. If you guys were trying to be incognito, you failed miserably."

"Oh. So. Did you then tell your mother we were in Atlanta? Because when she finds out she is going to hate me."

"I didn't tell her. It's hard for me to breach my allegiance with my grandmother, too."

"Then why'd you drag me out here?" I narrowed my eyes. "I thought you were going to fuss at me about bringing Miss Vivee here."

"No. I'm glad you're taking time with my grandmother," he said. "You know, sometimes she feels like she's losing her independence. We all hover over her, checking on her every second, trying to tell her what she can and can't do. I know that bothers her."

"She certainly never lets me question her independence. The way she bosses me around, there's never any uncertainty of who's in charge."

"I think it's okay to let her do whatever she wants. She's grown. But my mother, and sometimes Auntie Brie seem to forget that. They act like she's a child. My grandmother is sharp though, and smart. She doesn't need coddling. "

"Don't I know it," I said. "She's one of those people that could squeeze blood from a turnip. Since I've been around her, I've seen that whatever she sets her mind to accomplish she can do."

"Listen to you, 'squeeze blood from a turnip.' What do you know about those southern sayings?"

I laughed. "My grandparents are from the south. That's how I know to mind my manners with Miss Vivee. Plus, I see how she manipulates people to get what she wants. I've learned to just give in."

Bay laughed. "I know. She's like this chameleon. She gets to talking like she's a down home girl with the 'ain't' and 'cause' when she wants to give the impression she's just regular folk. Then she's got a different way when she's passing out her homemade remedies."

"I know," I said. "And then sometimes she's using all these big words like she's a college professor. But her lies –she can tell some big ones. Wow."

"She's not just acting, you know with the big words and all. She went to college."

"Really?"

"Yep. Got a degree in biology. Wanted to be a doctor."

"Wow. I didn't know that."

"Yeah. But what I'm trying to say is that my grandmother, sometimes when she's demanding, and seems, I don't know, obstinate, or mean, or overbearing, I think it's because she's fighting for her right to stay independent. You know? She has to be forceful to keep her personality. To be an 'adult.' Not to let people take over her life because they think she's old and helpless. You understand what I'm trying to say?"

"Yeah. I know," I said and looked back through the door of Kitty City. When I turned back around, Bay was staring at me. "Your mother explained to me once that as we grow old we still feel the same on the inside," I said, his staring weirding me out. "I know that Miss Vivee still wants to live her life." My words seemed to float right past him.

I let my eyes meet his, and his stare locked mine in. There was a twinkle there as if he was smiling at me through them. The moment then suddenly felt intense. I broke my gaze and the lingering silence between us became uncomfortable. I didn't like the feeling that sprung up in me from somewhere deep inside, out of nowhere. And then I decided I couldn't stay around Bay any longer.

I didn't know what he was doing to me.

"I probably should get back," I said breaking the silence. "I have to keep an eye on those two."

"So," he said. "I just came by to warn you to take good care of my grandmother and her boyfriend."

"That is not her boyfriend," I chuckled. "She says she is too old to have one of those." I kept my eyes away from looking into his. "So you came all the way up here to check on us?"

"No. I had to go to Gainesville for work."

Oh no. I hope that wasn't work that involved me.

"I-I thought you were on vacation? Your mother said you were going to be in Yasamee for a week, maybe longer," I said. "She said you were on vacation."

A smile lit up his face. "You asked my mother about me?"

"No." I lied and swallowed hard. "Not really. I mean . . . You know . . . It just came up."

"Oh," he said. "I am on vacation. But I had some evidence in my car that I needed to turn in."

"Oookaay." I didn't want to hear what that was about. "I gotta go," I said and ducked back inside of Kitty City before he could say anything else.

"She did good for herself," one of the strippers was saying when I sat back down at the table. I'm guessing from the size of her backside she was Buns Galore. "Didn't she, Champagne?" Buns asked the other girl who was wearing what looked like a gold lamé onesie.

"Yeah, she did. You should be proud of her," Champagne said. "She only worked here long enough to finish school."

"Finish school?" Miss Vivee asked. "I remember once she told me she wanted to be a cosmetologist."

"Oh, no. She did one better. She got herself a college degree."

"That's my girl," Miss Vivee clapped her hands together. "We're so proud of her, aren't we Mac?"

She should be on the stage somewhere, I thought. *This is definitely the kind of performance that would garner a Tony.*

"What did she study while she was in school?" Mac joined the masquerade. He and Miss Vivee were like two peas in a pod.

"She's a teacher. Up in Powder Springs."

"What grade does she teach?" Mac asked.

"Second graders," Buns said.

"Let me think," Champagne said. "I'll remember the name of the school. Hold on give me a minute . . ."

"It was Euclid Park Elementary," Buns spoke up. "Euclid. Like the mathematician."

Chapter Twenty-Nine
Powder Springs, Georgia

Thursday Morning, AGD

"She was a wonderful teacher. I really hated to see her go." Jill Sterba stood before us, her hands clasped in front of her. She spoke in a soft, even voice that was probably reserved for children and meddling nonagenarians. "But other than that, I really can't say anything."

Jill Sterba was the bespectacled, blonde-haired principal of Euclid Park Elementary School. She was tall and thin, and had a no nonsense air about her. She stood by the set of glass doors where she'd let us in, but it appeared that's all the far she was letting us go.

Just like no one thought it strange that Grandma and Grandpa Big Time Liars were in a strip club, no one gave it a second thought that a stripper called

Buns Galore knew that Euclid was a Greek mathematician. The school named in his honor was a one-story, tan brick building that housed grades kindergarten through third.

We had spent the night before in a five-star hotel in Atlanta that Miss Vivee paid for on her American Express Blue. Bay had left, thank God, and Miss Vivee insisted that she and I share a room. She also insisted that Mac had to get his own room, which she said he had to pay for, too. Then she spent all evening in his room with him. I stayed in our room and watched a movie and ordered room service. I wasn't going to let Miss Vivee pick up the charges for my food with the room, though. Although she was throwing money around like she was Oprah, she was still just a little old lady. Plus, I figured that Renmar had to have something to do with payments on that credit card.

Miss Vivee came back to our room late, well after I had gone to sleep. She must have just taken a "catnap" as my grandmother says, because as soon as the sun came up, so did she. I had to keep her calm until the school was open, because she was ready to go at dawn.

Miss Vivee had explained to Ms. Sterba that she and Mac were Gemma's long lost grandparents and that I was their nurse and companion.

More lies to keep up with. I was thinking about starting my own notebook just to help me keep track.

But the two of them finagled their way into her office by playing on Mac's bad leg. Good thing he'd brought his cane along.

"How can I help you?" she said and gestured toward two chairs that sat in front of her desk. I remained standing and leaned on a nearby wall.

"We just need some information," Miss Vivee said.

"Gemma didn't leave a forwarding address, working phone number or any emergency contacts. So, as I told you Mrs.-"

"Whitson," Mac said at the same time that Miss Vivee said "Pennywell."

They looked at each other. "Pennywell-Whitson," Miss Vivee said. It's hyphenated."

Principal Sterba nodded.

"So no way to contact our Gemma, huh?" Miss Vivee said. She reached out for Mac.

"It's okay, honey. We'll find her." He patted her hand and looked at Principal Sterba. "It's just that we can't find her anywhere. I really don't know if my poor wife can take anymore disappointment. We've been everywhere looking for her."

"Did you, uhm, try Atlanta," the principal seemed reluctant to say anything.

"Oh, yes," Mac said. "We know all about her life there. But nothing is more important to us right now then finding our grandchild."

"We know you can't give us any personal information like where she lived or anything." Miss Vivee bowed her head and lifted just her eyes. "But is there *anything* that you can tell us?" I could have sworn that I saw tears well-up in Miss Vivee's eyes.

Mac, on cue, grabbed her hand and this time rubbed it gently. "We're just so worried about her," he said to Principal Sterba. "She's all the family we've got left." He looked at Miss Vivee lovingly and she returned the gaze.

I swear, those two were the biggest liars. And it just seemed to come so naturally. *I wonder are all old people like that?* My grandparents are always telling some kind of story to us about what our parents had done when they were young or things that had happened to them. From now on, I'm taking everything they say with a grain of salt.

"Well, when Gemma first arrived here," Principal Sterba began her story about Gemma. Evidently Miss Vivee and Mac had been believable enough that she was willing to tell what she knew. "She had just graduated. She completed her student teaching in Marietta but said she wanted to live here in Powder Springs. Then she told me 'how' she worked her way through school." She put air quotes around the word "how."

"I was leery about hiring her at first," Jill Sterba said, her eyes showing that she was remembering the incident. "Of course we have a reputation to uphold and we want only the best environment for our students. But Gemma promised me that nothing would come back to haunt her or put the school in any bad light. She said that she'd never taken any pictures or been on the Internet, she was sure of that. Plus she worked under a stage name and always wore a black wig and heavy makeup. Even though a scandal would be devastating to our small school, I took her at her word and hired her.

"Gemma turned out to be a caring and dedicated teacher. The children and staff loved her. It wasn't long before she proved to me that I had made the right decision in giving her a chance. Then, one day, just out of the blue, she quit. She said that she wanted to keep her promise to me and something had come up where she didn't think she'd be able to.

"I knew that she must be referring to her days working in Atlanta so I didn't say anything. Didn't ask any questions. I accepted her resignation and she left. I did hear, later that is, that she had moved back home."

"Back home . . ." Miss Vivee let her voice trail off then she grabbed her dress over her heart, pulled it tight and looked at fake grandpa. "Mac, do you suppose . . ."

Mac's eyes got big. I don't know if he was playing along and seemingly understood what she meant, or if he really didn't know what it was he was "supposed" to know.

"Oh my," Miss Vivee started to fan her hand over her face. "There was a place that she used to run away to when she was young," she licked her lips and let her eyes move from Mac back to Principal Sterba. "Just to get away, you know. She always called it her other 'home.' I wonder . . ." Miss Vivee bowed her hand.

"Don't cry, Vivee. We'll find her. That's gotta be where she is," Mac said. "C'mon, honey." He stood up and helped Miss Vivee stand.

"Thank you so much, Principal Sterba," Miss Vivee said through fake sniffles.

"Call me, Jill," the principal told her.

"Jill." Miss Vivee dabbed at her eyes with a hanky that Mac had produced from his pocket. "I think we now might just know where to find our Gemma."

I didn't want to be morbid, but I knew where to find Gemma, too. At the coroner's office in Augusta.

"Mac shake the woman's hand," Miss Vivee said. "I think she may have just given us back our granddaughter."

Mac obliged. The crap flowing in the room was getting too deep for me to stay without wading boots so I slipped out into the hallway. Thought I'd go make a call to Hollywood and find an agent for Miss Vivee. That woman had definitely missed her calling.

Chapter Thirty
Yasamee, Georgia

Thursday Afternoon, AGD

No one in Atlanta that we talked to knew a Jeffrey Beck. Principal Sterba said Gemma left no contact numbers or information on next of kin. That meant she had no names or addresses to share with us. The strippers, Miss Vivee found out when I was outside talking to Bay, did seem to think that Gemma had two boyfriends. Maybe Jeffrey Beck was one of them, but we weren't able to confirm it and we hadn't a clue who the other one could be and that worried Miss Vivee. She couldn't "connect the dots," she kept saying, if she didn't have all the information.

With Miss Vivee being the Queen of Lies, and her trusty cohort, Sir Mac, seconding every fib she told I was beginning to think that Miss Vivee might could wrangle enough information out of her unsuspecting suspects to find out "whodunit." So it made me sympathetic when she was upset about not finding Jeffery Beck, or the name of the second man in Gemma's life.

"I know what we have to do," she said with some reluctance in her voice. I'm sure she wasn't timid about asking me to do anything, I couldn't ever get out of anything she wanted me to do. I just think her hesitation stemmed from the fact that she wasn't sure what her next step in her crime solving spree would be.

"What is it, Miss Vivee? Who do we have to lie to now?"

"Lie? We haven't lied to anyone," she said sounding affronted.

"We've lied to *everyone*, Miss Vivee." I bit back a laugh. "Well. *You've* lied to everyone."

"You just don't understand the art of investigation," she said her nose wrinkled intimating I was confused. "Ask Bay. You have to create an environment where the people you question feel comfortable. Willing to talk. That's all I did."

"Uh-huh," I said narrowing my eyes. "Yeah. Right. Who do you want to question in your 'comfortable environment' now?"

"I want to talk to Koryn Razner. Gemma's houseguest."

Why wasn't I surprised?

"With all of other suspects so far away," I said. "It's looking more and more likely Home Girl is our killer. You sure you want to talk to her?" I made sure she could detect the concern in my voice. "Maybe let the Sheriff do it."

"He already talked to her. Remember? He got nothing. And she's not the killer."

"How do you know?"

"Because she's still in town. Still going to Viola Rose's on Saturdays." She shook her head and set her mouth in a tight line. "I just can't see it unless she's some kind of deranged, hardcore sociopath, psycho-killer. No feelings. No remorse."

"Maybe she is."

"I'd be willing to bet a fat man that she's not."

I hadn't seen any fat men in Yasamee since I'd arrived. I was thinking that perhaps Miss Vivee had lost them all with her penchant for placing ill-conceived bets.

Nonetheless, lies, bad bets, and all, I had become quite fond of Miss Vivee and her antics, I hadn't heard from my mother with the go-ahead to work legitimately on the Island, so I agreed to take her to talk to Miss Psycho-Killer.

Chapter Thirty-One

This time, I decided, I was going in Gemma Burke's house with Miss Vivee. That way I could at least try to keep her activities on the right side of the law.

We drove over to see Koryn in my jeep, in virtual silence. I didn't know if Miss Vivee was mad at me because I refused to drive that boat she called a car, or if she was quiet because she was thinking hard on something. Cat was stretched across the back seat, not a care in the world. I turned on the radio and listened to Whitney Houston's *How Will I Know* while I drove the two miles from the Maypop to Koryn's.

The windows on the front of Gemma's house were open. A breeze flowing through ruffled the white sheer curtains. A "Home" doormat sat in front of a canary blue door with a gold knocker. Two

Adirondack chairs that matched the blue on the door were sitting on the front porch. And Miss Psycho-Killer herself was sitting in one of them. Feet up on the banister, Koryn was wearing a pair of cut off shorts and a halter. She was reading a book of poetry, and sipping on a glass of iced tea.

The scene certainly didn't paint the picture of a day in the life of a murderer.

Maybe Miss Vivee was right.

I parked one house up. Miss Vivee said she didn't want Koryn to "turn tail" and run because we pulled up into the driveway, and I didn't want to park right in front of the house, either.

As usual, Miss Vivee didn't fill me in on the strategy she was using to elicit the smoking gun that would find us our actual killer. I was supposed to be the wingman, but I was more like a bat on our little capers, always flying in the dark.

I got out the car and then helped Miss Vivee and Cat out. We walked up to the porch.

"Hello," Miss Vivee said.

I wondered what lies she had set to tell.

"I'm Miss Vivee and this is Logan. We wanted to speak to you about Gemma."

Well would wonders never cease? She told the truth.

"Hi," Koryn said. "Come on up and have a seat." She set her glass of iced tea on the floor of the porch. "I can get another chair from the house." She stood up and pointed toward the door. "And get you something to drink? Some iced tea?"

"That's okay," I said. "I can stand."

"You sure?" she asked.

"Yep. I'm good. Thanks."

"She's fine," Miss Vivee said with a wave of her hand and sat down in the other Adirondack chair. "And we don't need anything to drink. Thanks for offering, though."

Cat went up to Koryn and gave a sniff. Koryn bent down, putting her nose into Cat's face, she ruffled the hair around her neck. Patting her on her head, Koryn said. "Good dog," and looked at Miss Vivee. "What's her name?"

"Cat."

Koryn let out a gentle laugh and gave Cat one more pat.

"So what did you want to know?" She had a soft voice and easy demeanor. Dressed for a lazy summer afternoon, she was barefoot and had her brown hair, with its haphazard cut, pulled back in a ponytail. Strands of it fell down around her face and neck.

"Gemma Burke was murdered." Miss Vivee said, taking off her sunglasses. No fanfare. No preamble.

She announced it like she was reading the day's menu at the Maypop.

When she goes for honesty, she turns it on full force.

"I know," she said. "I heard talk at the Jellybean Café." She pulled her knees up to her chest and put her feet on the chair. "I guess she was poisoned? Although when I asked the Sheriff about that he said he wasn't at liberty to discuss it. He'd just come by because he heard there'd been a disturbance. I told him everything was okay and he left."

"He's right. He'd compromise the investigation if he discussed it," Miss Vivee said. "But I can tell you this, Gemma wasn't poisoned."

"She wasn't?" she asked. She put her feet down and leaned forward. "Then how was she killed?"

"We're working on that." Miss Vivee said matter-of-factly.

"*You* are?" Koryn had a surprised look on her face. She looked at me and then back to Miss Vivee. "Why?"

"The Sheriff asked us to help."

Now the lies begin.

"He had to work with the coroner's office up in Augusta to get the body autopsied," Miss Vivee said without even flinching. "But because I know everyone in town, he asked me to think about who might have

215

done it." Miss Vivee patted her leg and Cat jumped up in her lap. Stroking him she said, "Me coming to talk to you is probably a little more than what the Sheriff had in mind when he asked me, but something Gemma Burke said to me right before she died got me thinking. I thought I'd come over and speak with you about it."

I looked at Miss Vivee and just shook my head.

"I'll do whatever I can to help find who did this," Koryn said. "Gemma saved my life. I wish I could do more than just answer questions now." She looked down at her hands. "*After* she's gone."

"How did Gemma save your life?" I asked. But as soon as I did, Miss Vivee furrowed her brows and gave me a scolding look that said "I'm asking the questions."

"I was in an abusive relationship," Koryn said seemingly unaware of Miss Vivee's displeasure. "Very abusive." She looked at me. "I feared for my life. And Gemma understood. She'd been in an abusive relationship, too. Not as bad a mine, but it made her understand what to do to help me. She brought me down here with her. Sort of let me hide out here." A slight smiled crossed her face. "She'd said no one I knew would come to Yasamee. I'd be safe."

"And that's exactly what she said to me," Miss Vivee said. "And then she told me about two men in her life. One breaking her heart, and the other trying to break the bones in her body."

The lies were growing exponentially.

"She said that to you?" Koryn looked at Miss Vivee in disbelief. "She really didn't like to talk about that kind of stuff."

"She told me," Miss Vivee said, gentleness showing in her voice. "People in this town often come to me." She reached over and squeezed Koryn's hand. "When they need someone to talk to. I've lived a long time. Seen a lot of things." She looked Koryn in the eye. "Been through a lot of things myself."

"Well. I know that Darius never broke any of her bones," Koryn said.

Ah, his name is Darius.

Miss Vivee winked at me on the sly, then said, "I think she just used that word metaphorically."

I had to try really hard not to roll my eyes.

Koryn nodded.

"But I know that Darius is who she was talking about when she said the part about breaking bones because she told me so," Miss Vivee said. "And Jeffrey Beck is the one that broke her heart."

Koryn lifted her eyebrows and sat back in the chair. "Gemma told you all of that?"

Miss Vivee nodded her head.

"I mean, I believe you because you know their names, and what happened – basically – but she never wanted to talk about that. I'm surprised she told you."

"Well she did," Miss Vivee assured her. "But you know, Koryn, with love often comes trouble." Koryn nodded her head. "And as you've experienced that trouble can cause great harm. Not just to your heart."

"I know," she said and rubbed her arm. "So you think that maybe Darius or Jeffrey killed her?"

"Well, you know," Miss Vivee said. "It's for Sheriff Haynes to put all the clues together and deduce who the culprit is. But the more information he has, the better shot he has on solving this whole thing."

Koryn nodded eagerly. She set forward. "Darius was here the day she died," she said. "Does the Sheriff know that?"

"In Yasamee?" I asked, my eyes wide.

"Yeah," she said. "He'd come because he'd been trying to blackmail her."

Chapter Thirty-Two

Koryn telling us that Darius was trying to blackmail Gemma made a big, wide crack in a case that I think even Miss Vivee was beginning to believe wouldn't ever be solved.

Miss Vivee's jaw went slack and she did one of her "lost in the moment" gazes over the banister and out in the street.

"How do you know he was in Yasamee?" I asked.

"He came by the house. Said he was looking for Gemma. I didn't know who he was, but I'm not really trusting of men nowadays so I didn't want to tell him anything," she said. She took in a deep breath. "I told him she wasn't home and I didn't expect her back anytime soon. He told me to tell her that 'Darius' came by to see her and that he wasn't planning on leaving until he talked to her."

"Did he talk to her?" I asked.

"I'm not sure. He stayed parked out in front of the house for a little while. Not too long. But long enough that it worried me. He was in a blue truck," she said her eyes drifting off. "If I'd known Gemma wasn't poisoned by the bouillabaisse, I would have told the sheriff about him being here." She looked at me. "I never thought he had anything to do with it." She licked her lips. "I didn't go out while he was here, but I kept peeking through the curtains until he left." She looked down at her hands. "Gemma never did come back home."

"Did Gemma tell you that Darius was blackmailing her?" I asked. I couldn't help asking a question or two of my own.

"Yeah. That's why she moved back here. I don't think that he ever did actually blackmail her. He tried to but she said that she took the wind out of his sail."

"What does that mean?" I asked.

"That means whatever it was he had against her, she fixed it so he couldn't use it against her anymore," Miss Vivee said. "That makes me think that whatever he was trying to blackmail her about was the reason she left Euclid Park Elementary School."

"She taught second grade there," Koryn said. "She loved that job. I felt so bad when she left it. I didn't want her to do that for me."

"I don't think she did it for you, Koryn," Miss Vivee said. "I think she did it to keep her promise to the principal there. Jill Sterba." Miss Vivee, with lips pulled tight, stared at me for a long minute.

I nodded at Miss Vivee. "Koryn, do you know Darius' last name?" I asked. "Gemma only told Miss Vivee his first name. And I'm sure the Sheriff would want to talk to him."

Miss Vivee's lying must be contagious.

"It's Hamilton," Koryn said.

"Darius Hamilton," Miss Vivee said. She seemed to be committing the name to memory.

"And he lives in South Carolina now. Right across the Savannah River Gemma told me," Koryn was talking fast. She seemed ready to share all the information she knew. "I remember her saying that now it didn't matter, wherever he lived, he couldn't hurt her anymore."

"Do you know where in South Carolina?" Miss Vivee asked.

"No. She never told me. I know that that's where he grew up, though. She said he was running home to his daddy. I think his father was pretty famous in whatever city it is where they lived." She looked at Miss Vivee. "You think that'll help the Sheriff?"

"Oh. I know it will," she said. She stood up. "C'mon, Logan. We've got to find Sheriff Haynes right away and give him the information that Koryn has given us." Miss Vivee stood and that prompted Koryn to get up, too."

"I'm so glad I could help," she said her eyes beaming. "Gemma was so nice to me. She hardly knew me and she offered to help me." She looked back toward the house and put her hands in her short's back pocket. "I really don't know what I'm going to do now."

"We'll figure out something," Miss Vivee said. "We'll stop in and see you again before too long." Miss Vivee patted Koryn on the arm and headed down the steps. "C'mon Cat," she said. The dog had gone back to Koryn for more patting before leaving.

"I love your dog, Miss Vivee." Koryn smiled. "Cat. Such a crazy name for a dog."

"She likes it," Miss Vivee said, holding onto the banister.

"Bye," I said. "And thanks for talking to us."

"No problem," Koryn said and waved.

I got Miss Vivee and Cat in the car. Coming around to the driver's side, I glanced back up at the house. Koryn had gone inside. Her book lying open, face down to save her page. The glass of iced tea sitting by the chair.

I kind of felt sorry for her. Having to be on the run. All of her help gone. She'd probably have to move soon. No more Shepard's pie Saturdays at the Jellybean Café for her.

I got in the car, put my seatbelt on and looked at Miss Vivee. "Well." I reached over and buckled her in. "What do we do now? Darius Hamilton is in South Carolina and we can't go there." I tried to enforce that fact right away. "And we still don't know where Jeffrey or Miranda Beck are, so . . ."

While I talked, Miss Vivee pulled out her notebook and wrote something down. A time or two, she looked back up at the house and then would write something else. Finally, she put the notebook back and pulled out her sunglasses and said. "C'mon. Let's go."

"Okay," I said starting the car. "Where to?"

"Home," she said put on her sunglasses. "We have to tell Lloyd Haynes what we found out."

"Oh," I said almost in shock. "You really are going to tell the sheriff?"

"What do you want to do?" She turned and looked at me. "Grab a couple of guns, a six pack of beer, ride to South Carolina and have a shoot-out?"

Chapter Thirty-Three

Miss Vivee didn't wait until we got back to the Maypop to call the Sheriff. She had me call him from my iPhone and told him to meet us at the bed and breakfast as soon as he could.

We hadn't been back more than fifteen minutes when he showed up. Bay Colquett came in right after.

Who called him?

We were all in the foyer. Miss Vivee and I sat in our usual place – on the tufted bench. Brie sat behind the counter and Renmar stood next to it.

The sheriff took off his hat when he came through the door. He looked around the room, nodded his head and ran his fingers through his hair that had fallen in his face.

"We got the autopsy report back," he said. He looked over at Miss Vivee and snorted in a breath. He paused, not saying anything for a long minute. His silence made my heart skip a beat.

So how did she die? The question was on a loop in my brain the whole time we waited for him to say.

Sheriff Haynes swung his eyes to Renmar. "Gemma wasn't poisoned," he announced finally.

As soon as he said it, Miss Vivee hit me on my knee and pushed a grin through the wrinkles in her face. Renmar must have been holding her breath, because she let out a long sigh.

"Miss Vivee," the Sheriff said. "I might as well let you be the one to say it. Just got the report over the fax right when you called me. But you seemed to know what it would say even before we took Gemma's body up to Augusta."

"What is he talking about, Mother?" Renmar said.

"Gemma Burke dry drowned," Miss Vivee said. She seemed beside herself with joy over being right. "More than likely the autopsy showed that the right side of her diaphragm was ruptured."

Everyone looked at the Sheriff to see if he was going to confirm.

"Yes it was," he said. "That's why she was coughing and complained of chest pains. The ME said it probably happened about an hour before she died." He licked his lips and looked at Miss Vivee. "I'm guessing you got something else? That's why you called?"

"I may have the name of the murderer."

"Mother!" Renmar said at the same time Brie said, "Momma!"

Brie came over and wiggled her hips, making room for her to sit on the end of our bench. Miss Vivee moved over to let her in..

She smiled at Miss Vivee "How do you know this, Momma?" Brie said.

Miss Vivee looked at me and then up at the Sheriff. "Koryn Razner told me."

"Who is that?" Renmar and Brie said almost in unison.

"Who is it, Grandmother? What's the name of the person that Koryn Razner gave you?" Bay spoke for the first time, interrupting Renmar and Brie's questioning.

"His name is Darius Hamilton," she said. "He lives in South Carolina. Don't know what city, but I'm thinking it's not far. His father may be a politician or prominent citizen. That might make him easier to find. And I think there may have been previous episodes of violence between him and Gemma Burke."

"Momma!" Brie said. "What in the world!" She was grinning ear to ear. But Renmar seemed upset.

"Mother. What have you been doing? Is this what all this running around with Logan was all about? Getting information on Gemma's death?"

Miss Vivee sucked her teeth. "Don't be silly, Renmar. Of course it wasn't. You think Logan would let me do something like that?" Renmar eyed me. "She took me to church, the cemetery and to the diner, just like I told you, stuffing me to the brim with Viola Rose's horrid egg salad every time we went. And," Miss Vivee put her head down and lowered her voice. I could feel an Oscar worthy performance coming on. "I didn't want anyone to know, but she took me to see Mac."

"Mac?" Brie clapped her hands. "That's so good, Momma! I'm so glad you're getting out and spending time with your friends. Renmar, isn't that good?" Brie took Miss Vivee's hand. "We were getting so worried about you wasting away in this house."

Renmar stood with her mouth opened. She put her hands on her hips. "I thought you loved Viola Rose's egg salad."

"No one makes it like you, Renmar." Miss Vivee said smiling.

"Enough about egg salad," Bay said, his voice stern. He probably knew that none of what Miss Vivee said was true, but he didn't say anything. "We're going to have to find this Darius Hamilton and have a talk with him. Whatever was speculated before," he looked at the Sheriff and then his mother, "that autopsy report made it clear. Gemma Burke's cause of death has been officially classified as homicide."

Chapter Thirty-Four

Thursday Evening, AGD

I was sitting on the front porch minding my own business and for once, since first coming to Yasamee, not involved in any crimes or untruths when FBI Guy cornered me.

"What have you been doing with my grandmother?" he asked me.

"What?" I said my eyes big. "Haven't we gone over this before? I'm not doing anything with her." I scooted over as he muscled his way onto the swing where I was sitting. "And if you think that I've been manipulating Vivienne Pennywell," I continued visibly irritated. "You don't know your grandmother very well. She doesn't let anyone do anything to her. She is always in control."

He didn't say anything for a while. Then he looked at me. "What is it between you and my grandmother? She took to you like a moth to a flame."

"I haven't any idea why she decided she liked me. It might have had something to do with her liking the idea that my mother thinks people are from Mars." I gave him a sideways glance. "Believe me, though. I did not encourage her taking to me."

"Your mother thinks what?"

Thank goodness he didn't know anything about that.

"Nothing," I said and licked my lips. "Your grandmother told me I had to help her. So I really didn't have any choice. Even though at that time I didn't know her very well, I didn't want to be rude and say no to her." I lowered my head and glanced at him through the corner of my eye. "Plus," I fiddled with my fingers, "I was afraid she would turn me over to you if I didn't."

"Turn you *over*?" His eyes lit up. "Oh. Have me turn you *in*. Because it was you-"

"I don't want to talk about it," I said waving him off. "Whatever I've done in the past, I have more than made amends by being nice to that little old lady in there," I pointed toward the inside of the house. "Even if I did enjoy it. And," I emphasized, "by helping solve a crime."

"Speaking of which, I just got off of a call with Sheriff Haynes. He found Darius Hamilton. He lives in Melborne, South Carolina. Just across the border from Augusta. And it looks like he's got a record. Not much of one, but still he looks more and more like our guy."

"You found that out quickly," I said. "So, he's going to pick him up?"

"He can't pick him up, yet. We don't know if he did anything or not. Sheriff just wants to talk to him. Actually," Bay said, "he wants me to talk to him. Lloyd doesn't have any experience with this kind of stuff. People don't get murdered in Yasamee."

"Oh and do you have experience with that kind of 'stuff'?" I asked. "Talking to murderers?"

"I have experience interrogating all kinds of criminals," he said and winked.

"Oh," I squeaked out in a cough. I shifted my body on the swing and inched down away from Bay. "Maybe we should talk about that . . ."

"Don't worry about it. You're cool."

"Really?" I said. Then I furrowed my brow. "You're just going to forget about it?"

"About what?" he said, a mischievous smile crossed his face.

"Nothing."

He said don't worry about it so I was going to drop it. Let sleeping dogs lie, like my grandmother used to always say. I drew my lips in tight and held them.

"My grandmother likes you," Bay said. "I know I said this before, but you helped her. That means a lot to me." His eyes locked with mine and I could feel a small army of butterflies try to take flight in my stomach. "Miss Vivee is very special to me," he said, his voice soft and low. "And anyone that's okay with her is okay with me."

"Thanks" I said and averted my eyes away from his. "I think."

"And . . ." he said, drawing out the word. "I'm also letting it slide because you're riding with me up to Melborne."

"No I'm not!" I screeched. "Uh-uh. No way." I folded my arms across my chest.

Why in the world would he think I'd go somewhere with him?

"Why not?"

"For one thing Darius Hamilton is a psycho-killer. I go up there, and there might be a shoot-out. I'm not trying to be in the middle of that."

"We're just going to talk to him. There is *not* going to be any shoot out." He grinned. "And if there was, I could protect you."

"Please. Isn't it against the rules or something for the FBI to take civilians while trailing a killer?"

"Darius Hamilton's father is the former mayor of Melborne and is now a lawyer. His grandfather was a state senator. Lloyd told me that when he talked to the law enforcement officers over there they were very helpful. They said that Darius' family would be helpful too, and that there wouldn't be any problems."

I shook my head the entire time he was talking. Even if he wasn't going to turn me in for trespassing at Track Rock Gap, and no one was going to shoot anyone over in Melborne, I did not want to go anywhere with him. Ever.

"My grandmother wants you to go with me," he said.

"She does not." Bay must of inherited Miss Vivee proclivity for lying.

"Yes she does. And she told me not to take 'No' as an answer from you."

"Is lying in your family's genes? They just roll off of Miss Vivee's tongue. Your mother . . ." I eyed him. "I don't mean anything disrespectful about your mother. But she seems to not like telling the truth either, and now you."

"You don't like my family?"

"Yes. I like your family. I'm just saying."

"C'mon," he bumped his shoulder against mine. "Go with me. It'll be fun."

"My idea of fun is not hunting down killers. I like digging in dirt."

"I could help you get permission to dig over at the Island," he said. "It's part of the federal-"

"I know what it's a part of. And I already have help. Thanks."

"What about this?" He pushed out his bottom lip and made puppy dog eyes then pointed to his face. "It always worked with my grandmother. I made this face. I got my way."

I laughed. "I don't believe Miss Vivee would ever fall for anything that pathetic."

"My grandmother's a push over. And we're very close." He eyed me. "Nothing she wouldn't do for me. When I was little I spent all my time with her. She taught me all about her voodoo herbs."

"Did she now?"

"Yeah. So if I wanted to, I could *make* you go to Melborne with me. In fact I could make you break out in boils. Even throw up frogs." He wiggled his eyebrows. "All I'd have to do is go back to her greenhouse and whip up a quick little potion."

"You are scaring me." I laughed.

"So you'll go?"

I started shaking my head again. "No. No, I won't go. Nope. No way. No." I pointed my finger at him "And here's another one for you, just for good measure. No."

"Fine. You leave me no alternative." His voice switched to a low, slow southern drawl. "I'mma go and fetch my handcuffs from inside." He jerked his thumb toward the house and gave a nod. "And then me and you are gonna take a ride up to Gainesville."

I narrowed my eyes and took in a breath. "You are an evil man," I said, my voice low. "Fine." I held my hands up in surrender. "I'll go."

Chapter Thirty-Five

Friday Morning, AGD

Miss Vivee was extra nice to me (not that she'd ever been even a little nice to me before) when she found out I was going with Bay to South Carolina. She tried to tell me what to wear and how to comb my hair.

"Miss Vivee," I said. "We're going to catch a killer not to prom. I don't have to get all made up."

We were sitting in the dining room. I was waiting for Bay and the Sheriff. They had decided to take two cars. The Sheriff would take his car in case they were bringing Darius back to put him in jail. And Bay would take his car for the two of us. I was not looking forward to riding with Bay for the hour or so there and then that same time back.

"Well you look like you're on your way to hike up a hill. I was thinking you could charm a confession

236

out of that Darius Hamilton," Miss Vivee said. She puckered up her lips. "You'd need on a little lipstick for that." She held up her tube of the pink she'd worn to the strip club.

I waved her hand away. "I don't know what you're up to Miss Vivee, but we both know that I'm not going to be doing any talking. I'm just going because your grandson, officer of the law that he is, blackmailed me into it."

"He did no such thing," she said.

"He did, too. He told me if I didn't go he'd take me back to Gainesville, toss me in jail, and throw away the key."

She laughed.

I don't know how she thought that was funny.

"It's not funny," I said. "You and your family are a bunch of criminals."

Bay walked in. "And who are *you* calling a criminal," he said.

"I didn't mean for you to hear me say that," I said.

"Leave her alone, Bay." Miss Vivee stood up. "Give your old grandmother a hug."

He happily obliged. But he was so tall he had to bend down almost halfway to hug her. "Mornin', Grandmother."

"Mornin.' Now you two, go catch a killer," Miss Vivee said patting his arm. "And you, Missy," she wagged a finger at me. "Call me as soon as Bay talks to that low-life killer. I want to know everything that happens."

"We'll call you, Grandmother," Bay said. "Don't worry."

"Thank you, Grandson," Miss Vivee said and pulled him back down, planting a kiss on his cheek.

"Okay," Bay said looking at me. "You ready?"

"Yep."

"Good," he said and smiled. "You look nice."

I looked down at my khaki cargo shorts, white tank top and tennis shoes. "Thanks," I said, tugging down on my baseball cap with "I ♥ to Dig" inscribed across the top. I winked at Miss Vivee.

We walked out to get in Bay's car and I noticed it was the same car my father had. A Cadillac SRX. Same make. Same model. Same color.

"Is this the car you've had since you've been down here?" I asked.

"Yep."

Why hadn't I noticed before?

"Is it your car?"

"Yeah," he said. "Why?"

Man, my daddy would love this. Me hanging out with a guy who has his same taste.

"No reason," I said and hopped in.

As soon as we hit the highway, I reached over and turned down the music. "So. I've been wondering," I said. "Why did you follow me down to Yasamee?"

"That's my job. I track down criminals."

I sucked my tongue against the roof of my mouth.

He tapped my arm. "I was just kidding."

I didn't say anything.

"I was already on my way to Yasamee." He glanced over at me and then back at the road, seemingly wanting to explain. "When I got the call to check out Track Rock Gap, I was already on my way to Yasamee for a visit."

"Really?" I laughed. "Nobody in the entire world would believe that. It's just too coincidental. You stopped in Gainesville where I just happened to be . . ." I looked at him. "Minding my own business, and then you just happened to come to Yasamee after I told you I was coming to Stallings Island?"

"Yep. I guess that's the way it happened. Although what you were doing at Track Rock Gap *is* technically my business."

I exhaled noisily. "That's too much of a coincidence."

"Maybe it wasn't coincidence." He glanced at me and smiled. "Maybe it was fate," he said.

"I'm in love with Colin Pritchard."

"The deputy?"

"Like your grandmother asked me once: 'Do you know another Colin Pritchard?'"

"No," he said. "I sure don't." He bit down on his lip. "But you're kidding, right?"

"Well that's the plan," I said. "Me be in love with him. He be in love with me. He doesn't know about my plan yet, though."

"Why do you have this plan?"

"Because I think he's cute," I said.

"In a dumb sort of way, right?"

I chuckled.

"What about me?" he asked. "You think I'm cute?"

"No."

"Yeah," he said nodding his head. "I'm definitely going to have to give a visit to Grandmother's greenhouse. Whip up a love potion."

"You'd never get me to drink that."

"I'd put it in one of my mother's fruit cups. She told me how you 'gobbled' those down. Or did she use the word 'demolished?' I can't remember the word, but I do remember envisioning a lion tearing into its prey, teeth ripping into flesh, ravaging on its remains."

"Oh my." I rubbed my hand across my forehead. "How embarrassing." I scrunched up my nose. "You know one of you are always telling me what the other one said. Do you guys sit and talk about me when I'm not around?"

"Yep. We do. My grandmother actually gave me the idea of cooking up a love potion the last time we talked about you," he said and started grinning.

"Speaking of potions, do you mind if I ask you a question."

"No. I don't mind." He glanced at me. "For you, I'm an open book."

"I was wondering about your father," I said ignoring his "open book" comment.

Miss Vivee had told me that she helped Louis Colquett "pass over," as she put it, when we got back from Atlanta just as she promised. But it was at his request she'd said. It wasn't that I didn't believe her, it was just that people thought Miss Vivee capable of such things, and I wanted to know what Bay thought, especially since he was being so "open" with me.

"Don't take this the wrong way," I said. "But what do you remember about your father's death?"

He shot a glance at me, then didn't say anything for a little while. "My father was in a lot of pain. He had cancer that just ravaged his body. Every breath he took hurt." He seemed to drift off in thought, his eyes maybe even misty.

"I know why you're asking," he said. "Some people say my grandmother killed him. But she loved him like he was her son. And I know that my grandmother, if she had it in her power, would never let him keep suffering like that. My mother, deep down somewhere knows that too. But when people accuse my grandmother of, well, uhm, you know, my mother defends her to the end." He looked at me. "One thing Miss Vivee taught me, especially since I was the only black kid around, was never to be ashamed of who you are. And she was certainly never ashamed to be the Voodoo Herbalist Priestess of Yasamee. And I'm glad she is because she used her powers to help my dad."

I nodded my head, but didn't say anything.

"So does that answer your question?"

"Yep," I said and smiled.

"Good," he said. "Now let's talk about us."

Us?

Thank goodness I was saved by the bell. Bay's phone rang just at that awkward moment. Looking at the screen he said, "It's the Sheriff." He swiped his finger across it to accept the call. "Hold on a second, let me get this."

While he spoke to the Sheriff I wondered what had gotten into him, all the flirting he was doing. And then I remembered how he always flashed that smirk of his when he'd talk to me.

It had been kind of flirtatious.

I adjusted myself in my seat and stared at him. His eyes on the road, concentrating on his phone call. *Hmmm . . .*

I let my eyes roam taking him in. I realized I never noticed how handsome he was. He had smooth, honey-colored skin, piercing hazel eyes, and long thick eyelashes. His close cut, coal black hair was wavy. *I wonder how it feels.* I lifted up my hand toward his head. He glanced at me. I put my hand back down. I watched him speaking into the phone, his full lips moving as he talked, suddenly it made me want to nibble – no – bite them and . . .

I listened as his spoke on the phone. His voice was so sultry. He pushed his tongue out and ran it slowly across his bottom lip . . .

Oh. My.

And he smells so good.

I leaned over, closed my eyes and sniffed. Mmmmm.

What is that?

When I opened my eyes he was looking at me, phone to ear, his scrunched up face asking "what's wrong with you?" I coughed pretending something was in my throat.

I shook my head. There definitely was no "us" and there never would be. I bit down on my own lip and

wondered how in the world I was going to get away
from him.

Chapter Thirty-Six
Melborne, South Carolina

"I don't know what you're talking about," he said. He sat at the end of the table in the interrogation room dressed in a gray T-shirt and blue jeans. He was leaning back, one leg pushed out straight, his arms crossed over his chest. His hair was scraggly, as was the stubble on his face. His skin was reddish from too much sun and he looked like he hadn't slept in a week.

Now he looked like a murderer to me.

We (as in me, too) were talking to Darius Hamilton, alleged killer of one Miss Gemma Burke. Only he was denying it with all the fervor of a man unjustly accused. The Sheriff's call to Bay had been to inform him that Former Mayor Daddy was bringing Naughty Killer Son over to the police station for questioning. We'd have the protection of the entire Melborne police department and Darius Hamilton's father.

Sheriff Haynes didn't go into the interrogation room with Bay. That was probably fine because if Darius was the killer, and he had fled over state lines, Bay as a federal officer had legal jurisdiction.

The Melborne sheriff really meant it when he told Sheriff Haynes that they would cooperate fully. That also meant I got to hear what Darius Hamilton had to say. Bay and I agreed that it was too bad that Miss Vivee hadn't come. She'd have been overjoyed to watch Gemma's murderer captured all thanks to her investigative work.

"We know you were in Yasamee last Friday." Bay locked eyes with him. "We also know that you tried to blackmail Gemma Burke," he spoke accusatorily.

Former Mayor Daddy was sitting in the small room behind the glass with me, the sheriffs and two other deputies. He let out a gasp as soon as the accusation came out of Bay's mouth about his son's criminal activity.

"Well, I didn't blackmail her. So tell her that it's not a crime to come to see a person."

"I can't tell her anything," Bay said.

"Well bring her in here," Darius said waving his arms around, "and I'll have my father tell her. He's a lawyer and he knows the law even if you people over in Yasamee don't."

Bay looked at the one-way mirror. He couldn't see through it, but it was obvious he was looking at us. He pulled out a chair and sat down. "Darius, you know why we're here. Let's not play games. Gemma is dead."

"Dead?" Darius's chair screeched across the floor as he pushed it back. He stood up and walked to a corner of the room. "No," he said and turned around looking at Bay pleadingly. "No. Not Gemma."

"She died last Friday."

"How?"

"I think you know how, Darius. And it would go a lot better for you if you just cooperated and tell me about it. I don't have time to play your little games."

Darius' eyes got wide. He walked back to his seat as if he were in a shock. "You think I killed her?" he said slowly. "I killed Gemma?"

"Yes you did. And I'm glad you're willing to admit it."

"No." His whole face frowned up. "I'm not admitting to anything. I didn't kill her."

"C'mon, Darius," Bay said and opened up the folder he had laid on the table. "Joy riding. Disorderly Conduct. Assault. Oh wait, those last charges never made it into court." Bay looked over at the mirror and it made Former Mayor Daddy fidget. "You've got a criminal record. Small things but then you stepped it up, didn't you? Looks like you having help getting out of trouble just led you to believe you could get away with whatever you wanted to do. Say for instance, murder?"

Darius' father huffed and puffed at Bay's line of questioning. The Sheriff of Melborne had to calm him down.

"None of those things say murderer," Darius protested and jabbed his finger on the folder. "And I am *not* a murderer." He hung his head, it seemed as if he was going to cry. "I loved Gemma. I would never hurt her."

"Tell me what happened when you spoke to Gemma in Yasamee," Bay said.

"I didn't talk to her."

"Come now, Darius. I have witnesses that say you came to Yasamee to talk to Gemma."

"Yeah. I did. But I didn't talk to her."

"What did you come to talk to her about?"

This time it was Darius who looked at the mirror. He knew his father was there listening and the look in his face said it pained him to have to disappoint him.

"You were right. I did try to blackmail her."

"How?"

"Gemma worked at a strip club up in Atlanta. That's how we met. And yeah, we had our fights, but what couple doesn't, you know?"

"I understand that," Bay said. "I know exactly how women are. Hard to get along with."

Was he talking about me?

Darius snorted out a laugh. "Yeah, so you understand. Like I said, we argued, but I never laid a hand on her. I did mean things to her, but I never hit her. Anyway," he sniffed, "she was just about finished with school when she met this guy. Jeffrey Beck. He was some big time financial analyst or something like that."

I took in a breath. Jeffrey Beck was the one person that Miss Vivee couldn't locate or find any information on.

"After she met him, she wanted to dump me. Said that she wanted a different life and he was the one to give it to her."

"Is that why you killed her."

"No!" His eyes wide, he said, "I didn't kill her. I'm telling you. But that's how I blackmailed her. She didn't know that this Mr. Fancy Pants charmer was married and had a kid. But I knew. I had followed her after she quit working at Kitty City. She moved to Powder Springs. And I used to watch her. Don't get me wrong, I'm no pervert. I just wanted to see her. Talk to her. Try to get her back. That's when I saw him."

He stopped talking and Bay prompted him to finish telling his story.

"So, how were you going to use that to blackmail her?"

"I was going to tell her principal."

I had a confused look on my face, as did everyone else standing in the room with me, but not Bay. He kept talking and asking questions just like he was on the same page as Darius.

"Go ahead," Bay said.

"His kid was going to the same school where Gemma worked. I saw him there once picking the kid up when I was there watching for Gemma."

"What was the name of the school?" Bay asked.

"Euclid Park. Gemma taught second grade, and Jeffrey's son, I found out, was in kindergarten. There's no way she could've kept her job if I told the school board that not only had she been a stripper back in Atlanta, but she was dating the married father of one of the students at the school. So I told her that if she came back to me, I wouldn't tell on her."

"That was clever, Darius."

"Yeah," he said. He closed his eyes and pulled his lips into a tight line. "But it backfired on me."

"How?"

"Gemma up and quit the school and left Powder Springs. She broke it off with Jeffrey and went back to Yasamee."

"So if you didn't have anything to blackmail her with, why did you go to Yasamee?"

"I told you. I loved her."

"Tell me what happened when you went to see her," Bay said.

"I went by her house but she wasn't there. I waited out front for five or ten minutes when I remembered that she jogged during the day. I didn't know where so I drove around until I found her."

"What time was that?"

"Oh. I don't know for sure. Around 11:45 or noon. Yeah, probably closer to twelve o'clock."

"Is that when you killed her."

"No!" Darius slammed his hand on the table so hard it made me jump. "Stop saying that. I didn't kill her."

"Okay," Bay said, not showing any emotion at all. "Tell me what happened."

"I found her at the park. She was talking to a guy. Tall. Dark hair. And they were having an argument. I watched from a distant, but I never got close to them."

"Was it Jeffrey Beck?" Bay asked.

"I'm not sure. But I think so. Anyway. They were having an argument. He seemed pretty mad, he hit his hand against a tree. I thought he was going to hit her."

"What did you do?"

"I left. I wasn't going to get in the middle of that."

"You hit women, but when you see them getting hit, you run?" Bay asked Darius.

"I told you!" Darius started yelling. "I never hit, Gemma."

"No," Bay said calmly. "You just killed her."

Chapter Thirty-Seven

Friday Evening, AGD

We all drove back to Yasamee the same way we went. Me and Bay in one car, and the Sheriff alone in his squad car. Darius Hamilton got to go home with his daddy.

The two sheriffs, Bay and Darius' lawyer/father talked long and hard about the evidence – or lack thereof – against Darius. No one could see that there was enough to bring him up on charges. And maybe it wasn't him that killed Gemma, Bay had to admit. Maybe it was the guy at the park.

"Jeffrey Beck," I said.

"Jeffrey Beck," Bay said and looked at me. "He is definitely a person of interest."

"I'ma call Miss Vivee," I said pulling out my iPhone. "And let her know what happened."

"Yeah, good idea," Bay said. "I just hope she won't be too disappointed about it." He glanced at me. "You know, that we didn't have enough to arrest Darius Hamilton."

"I just hope that she won't want to go out and get the evidence you need to arrest him." I raised an eyebrow. "Because I know she'll try and drag me along with her," I said as I punched in the Maypop number on my phone.

Miss Vivee picked up the phone on the first ring. I put my phone on speaker.

"Hi, Miss Vivee."

"Hi, Grandmother," Bay said.

"Hey you two. I could hardly sit still waiting for your call," she said. "Did you get that son-of-a-gun?"

I looked at Bay. "We didn't arrest him," I said.

"Why?" she shouted into the phone.

"You tell her," I whispered to Bay.

"We didn't have enough evidence against him, Grandmother."

"What in tarnation? How could you not? He was in town the day she died."

"Yeah, but according to his account." Bay said "He wasn't the only one in Yasamee that day."

"Who else was here?"

"Should I tell her?" Bay mouthed to me. I shook my head no.

"What? What you say," Miss Vivee said yelling.

"Jeffrey Beck might have been there," I said.

Bay's eyes got big. "I thought you didn't want to tell her?" he said in a voice just above a whisper. I hunched my shoulders.

"How do you know?" she asked.

So I told Miss Vivee the whole story as told to Bay by Darius Hamilton. All about the blackmail and the reason Gemma left teaching at Euclid Park. I told her about when he came to Yasamee and the argument he witnessed. And I told her that Bay and Sheriff Haynes were going to find Jeffrey Beck and talk to him, but that Darius wasn't completely off the hook. When I finished, Miss Vivee didn't say a word. She was so quiet it made me nervous.

I looked at Bay and then back down at the phone. "Miss Vivee, are you there?" I asked. "Are you okay?"

"Yes. Yes," she said. "I'm fine." Her voice was low and had started to trail off. "Well I'll let you two go. I don't like talking so much on the phone. I'll see you when you get back."

"Okay, Grandmother," Bay said.

"And Bay," she said.

"Yes."

"When you get back, make sure the Sheriff comes in with you."

"Okay, Grandmother."

"Okay now. Don't forget," she said.

"I won't."

I hung up the phone and looked at Bay. "What was that all about?"

"I don't know, but I'm worried about her," he said. "I know I gave that whole little speech to you when we were in Atlanta about her being independent and not coddling her. But right now, that's just what I want to do. I just feel like I wanna protect her. She sounded so sad. I don't want this making her feel sick or depressed."

"Me too," I said. "I'd feel so bad if she got sick about this. So, let's hurry up. Get back and make sure she'll be okay."

Riding with Bay to Melborne and back wasn't as bad as I'd thought. I enjoyed his conversation, and even though Miss Vivee was his grandmother, we shared the same concern about her. Bay called the Sheriff and told him to meet us at the Maypop, and we made it back as quick as we could. The Sheriff pulled up at the same time we did and we noticed there were a few cars out front.

The bell jangled over the oak doors as the three of us, Bay, Sheriff Haynes and I walked in. And there in the foyer were Renmar, Brie, Deputy Pritchard, Mac, Hazel and Oliver. And Miss Vivee was sitting on the bench we always shared, Cat lying at her feet.

"Is everything okay?" Bay asked looking around the room.

Renmar waved her hand in the air. "Mother made us all come in here and wait for you." She cut her eyes toward Miss Vivee and scowled. "She says she's solved Gemma's murder and we all had to be here for her to tell us who did it."

All of us looked at Miss Vivee.

"What do you know, Miss Vivee?" I asked and went over and sat next to her on the bench. "Was it Jeffrey Beck?" I didn't know how she could know that if that was what she was going to say. But she answered, "No."

"Then who," I asked. "Who killed Gemma Burke?

Miss Vivee pointed her finger to the person standing at the bottom of the steps. Their bruised hand resting on the banister.

"It was Colin Pritchard," she said. "He killed Gemma Burke."

Chapter Thirty-Eight

"I'm . . . The murderer?" Colin seemed confused. Even frightened. He spoke in short, quick sentences, taking a breath between words. His eyes darting around the room "No. No way. I'm . . . Not . . . I-I couldn't be." I saw a tear roll down his face as he started backing away toward the door. "I loved her." He looked over his shoulder at the entranceway, just as the sheriff stepped in front of it.

Miss Vivee leaned over and whispered to me. "Told you. That boy don't know his ass from a hole in the ground." Then she shouted at him, much louder than necessary, "Yes, Colin Pritchard, you are the murderer. Tell him Mac."

"Gemma died from blunt chest trauma. A diaphragmatic injury," Mac explained. The diaphragm is a muscle that allows the lungs to work. It relaxes so the lungs can fill up and pushes up to expel the air. When it doesn't work, because it's been ruptured like Gemma's, so Vivee tells me the autopsy found, then the person can't get in enough oxygen and they drown. It's called dry drowning."

"What are you talking about, Mac?" Colin said. "I didn't do anything to Gemma's diaphragm."

"The diaphragm can rupture from a fall or if struck with a firm object like a bat or a ball. Or a fist," Mac said balling up his hand and shaking it at Colin. "A fist to the abdomen, if the blow is hard enough, can burst a diaphragm."

Colin looked down at his hand and then his gaze drifted off.

"You remember that bandage you had on your hand the day Gemma died, don't you?" Miss Vivee asked Colin. "The bruise I brought salve for?"

My breath caught in the back of my throat.

Colin started shaking his head.

"You hurt your hand when you hit that tree, didn't you," Miss Vivee asked. "You were the one that Darius Hamilton saw arguing with Gemma in the park. You hit that tree with your fist. And you hit Gemma in her stomach."

Bay moved in closer to Colin and the Sheriff stood in front of the door and spread his legs shoulder width apart.

"Why is everyone looking at me?" Colin said. "I didn't do anything."

"You killed her, Colin," Hazel Cobb said, a look of realization on her face. "I remember that bandage. You killed Gemma Burke."

"I did not." His eyes darted around the room.

"How did you hurt your hand, Colin," Bay asked.

"We fought . . . I mean argued. Me and Gemma. I'll admit to that," Colin said. "And I did hit that tree with my fist." He rubbed his hand where the bandage had been. "I was just so upset. But she was fine when I left her."

"Tell us what happened," Bay said.

"She kept following me. First I went to Atlanta, then she came. I came back home and then she came back home. I wanted to know why. Why would she follow me around if she didn't want me? Why dump me and then taunt me?"

"She didn't dump you, Colin," Miss Vivee said.

"See, Miss Vivee, that's where you're wrong. She did." Colin closed his eyes and took in a sharp breath. "She knew I wanted her and she knew being around her would make me want her even more. So I just confronted her. I saw her out jogging and I asked her to come and talk to me. We walked to the park and I asked her why was she doing that to me and she said she wasn't following me. She said she didn't even think about me when she decided to move to Atlanta or back home. How could she say that? That's when we started arguing."

Tears started streaming down Colin's face. His voice deescalated to a whimper and he looked bewildered.

"Calm down, man," Bay said. "It's okay."

"I was just so mad, Bay. You understand, don't you?"

"Yeah, man. I understand."

"I was just so mad that I hit the tree. And then I had my fist balled up . . ." His eyelids started to flutter and he kept licking his lips. "And I was just saying 'Why,' you know?"

Bay said, "I know."

"And my fists were here." He put them in front of him. "And then I pulled them apart, real fast. You know, saying 'Why,' Not to hit her or anything."

Bay nodded.

"I pulled them apart too fast and . . . and Gemma was standing just to the front of me . . . On the side like here." He pointed to a spot, remembering what happened. "And my right fist hit Gemma in her side. On her right side. Right here." He pointed to the area on his own body. I hit her so hard. But . . . But . . . It was an accident."

"I know it was," Bay said.

"And then . . ." Colin looked at Bay, tears in his eyes. "And the force of me hitting her made her fall down those stone steps over at Mims Point Park. Just a couple," he said. "She only fell down a couple. She just hit them so hard. When she got up she was holding her side. I asked her was she okay. She said it just knocked the wind out of her. I asked her did she want me to help and she said just to leave her alone. I probably shouldn't have left her I know, but she told me to. And I was so mad at her." He shook his head as if he was trying to clear it. "I was so mad. I was even still mad at her when the Sheriff and I came here and she was dead. I didn't even care. How could I still be mad then?"

The Sheriff stepped forward and put handcuffs on Colin and he and Bay led him out the door. We could hear Colin saying through sobs, "I didn't mean to do it."

"Well, shut my mouth," Brie said with a giggle. "Colin is the one that killed Gemma and all this time I thought it was death by bouillabaisse."

"Brie!" Renmar said. "You really do need to shut your mouth. What an awful thing to say!" She put her hands up to her face. "And poor Colin. Really Brie, none of this is funny."

"Renmar, I hate to tell you," Miss Vivee said. "But until Logan and Bay told me that Darius Hamilton overheard the argument and saw the guy hitting his hand on a tree, I thought it was your bouillabaisse that killed her, too."

Epilogue

Saturday Morning, AB (After Bay)

My big, time-altering event was that I fell in love with Bay Colquett. It had taken exactly seven days from the time Gemma Burke died to the day that Miss Vivee solved her murder and in that time my life had been divided into two separate and distinct periods: *Before Bay (BB)* and *After Bay (AB)*. Although minute by minute what happened before he came into my life was slowly fading into a blur.

Won't my daddy be happy.

I know. Isn't it the weirdest thing? All along I thought I was attracted to Colin Pritchard and hated Bay Colquett. But thinking back on it, it was easy to see. I couldn't even ever think of anything to say to Colin. Our love affair was all in my head. But Bay, even though I thought he was going to arrest me, made it easy to talk to him. But what I think really made me sit up and take notice of Bay was the way he interrogated Darius Hamilton. He was so forceful and fierce. It made me tingle all over. Who doesn't like a man like that?

"I always just thought he was cute," I said defending myself. "I wasn't trying to move in with him."

"That's not what you told me," Bay said. I was sitting on his lap. He, Miss Vivee and I were sitting in the dining room when they had decided to tease me about "having eyes," as Miss Vivee put it, for Colin Pritchard, The Murderer.

"It's a good thing for your mother that you got me to look after you," Miss Vivee said. "Otherwise, I don't know what might've happen to you." Miss Vivee patted me on my knee and shook her head. "Bless your heart."

"I know what would have happened to her, Grandmother," Bay said and tugged at my ear. "She would have been filling out the visitation forms at the Brentwood Correctional Facility so she could visit her convict boyfriend and take prison pictures to post on Facebook."

"Oh yeah. You two are real funny," I said and hopped up off of Bay's leg. "But lucky for you both, I picked the right one in the end."

"You sure did," Miss Vivee said. "You couldn't ask for a better man than my grandson."

Miss Vivee was right about that, I thought, my eyes beaming. She had been right about so much. She knew from the start that Gemma had dry drowned. I found out that she and Mac had seen a case of a boy, years earlier that had died the same way. That's how they knew the symptoms.

And Miss Vivee made the right call when she said the sandstone steps at Mims Point Park could have been what killed her. It was actually the combination of the hard hit from Colin's fist and the fall that did it. But Miss Vivee knew that, too. And she said, she could tell by the injury to Colin's hand, when we told her that the person arguing with Gemma had hit the tree, that it couldn't be anyone but him.

Colin was being charged with involuntary manslaughter, which in the State of Georgia carried a prison term of one to ten years. He was standing trial though. He said that his actions weren't reckless and he couldn't have known what he did would cause Gemma's death, elements that must be proven to convict him. My uncle, Greg and my brother, Micah, both lawyers, agreed that if he got himself a good lawyer, he might could prove that in court and get off on the murder charges.

I was just glad I hadn't acted on the feelings I thought I had for him.

Everything had changed for me and I couldn't have been happier. I called my parents to tell them about Bay, and my mother told me she'd gotten me permission to start an excavation on the Island. *(Yay!)* Renmar and Oliver didn't seem too happy about that (I still didn't know what their conspiratorial actions were all about). But Renmar was happy that I was staying on at the Maypop, as was Koryn Razner.

Miss Vivee had given her a room so she could stay at the Maypop until she got on her feet, which probably wouldn't be long because Viola Rose and her husband, Gus, had offered her a job at the Jellybean Café.

Bay was going back to work, but he wouldn't ever be too far, he had promised. Sometimes, I hate to say it out loud, but crime does pay. Because of me trespassing at Track Rock Gap, I found the best FBI guy in all of Georgia. *Nay*, in the entire world, who I wouldn't mind if he kept me in his custody forever.

The End

Thank you for taking time to read *Bed & Breakfast Bedlam*. Look for other books in the Logan Dickerson Cozy Mystery Series. If you enjoyed this book, please consider telling your friends about it. And don't forget to take the time to click on the link and post a short review.
http://amzn.to/1y2Soyo

A Note from the Author

This is my first cozy mystery and I hope you enjoyed reading it as much as I did writing it. There are more to come, so be sure to follow Logan, Bay and Miss Vivee on their adventures – they'll be filled with mystery, murder and even a little romance.

Logan Dickerson is the daughter of the main character in my *Mars Origin "I" Series*. (So if you like mysteries with just a touch of sci-fi, you might want to check them out!). Logan is from Ohio (like me), but her stories are based in Georgia. I love the coastline there and thought it would be a perfect setting for a cozy mystery.

Some of the places in the book are real. Like Stallings Island and Track Rock Gap. The Maya invasion into North America is a theory proposed by some archaeologists and first seen by me on *America Unearthed* on the History Channel. Check it out. It's a fascinating theory. Yasamee, while a real Native American name, is a fictional place.

Thanks to all my beta readers: Kathryn Dionne, Dennis Whittaker, Erika Place, and Michael Lewis. The book is better because of you.

This book is dedicated to my granddaughter, Sydne. My red-headed girl is always full of interesting stories.

I appreciate all my reviews and look forward to reading what you thought about my book.

Grammatical errors are of course unintended, so if you find any, just email me and let me know what you've found.

I love connecting with my readers and look forward to chatting with you.

Read My Other Books

Coastal Cottage Calamity – A Logan Dickerson Cozy
Mystery
http://amzn.to/1SvL1Z4

Maya Mound Mayhem – A Logan Dickerson Cozy
Mystery
http://amzn.to/1fah16e

Food Fair Frenzy – A Logan Dickerson Cozy Mystery
http://amzn.to/2blGgne

Garden Gazebo Gallivant – A Logan Dickerson Cozy
Mystery
http://amzn.to/2blGgne

In the Beginning: Mars Origin "I" Series Book I
http://amzn.to/1cwDnd2

Irrefutable Proof: Mars Origin "I" Series Book II
http://amzn.to/1bwWjFt

Incarnate: Mars Origin "I" Series Book III
http://amzn.to/1y2Soyo

At the End of the Line
http://amzn.to/1fg7DYy

Mysticism and Myths
http://amzn.to/1tcCUCn

Coming Soon

Deep Delta Devilry – a Logan Dickerson Cozy
Mystery

A Lesson in Murder – A Logan Dickerson Cozy
Mystery

Angel Angst – A Normal Junction Cozy Mystery

Witches Wheel – A Normal Junction Cozy Mystery

Ghostly Gadfly – A Normal Junction Cozy Mystery

Get a FREE eBook of my first novel, *In the Beginning*, when you sign up for my newsletter. I'll never spam you, I promise, you'll just get updates on my books. Visit my website at www.abbyvandiver.com to get your book.

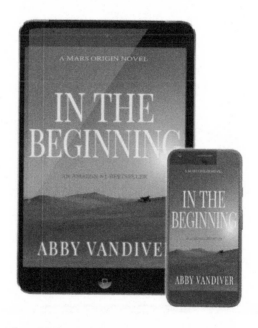

What if the history you learned in school wasn't the truth?

2,000 year old manuscripts, a reluctant archaeologists, a world changing discovery . . .
In the Beginning, an alternative history story.